INHERITING
THE
MISSING

BOOK 1 IN THE WINDCATCHER SERIES

Donald Hofstetter

TAZLINA GLACIER
PUBLISHING

First Edition, 2017
ISBN 978-0-9970058-3-7
Tazlina Glacier Publishing
PO Box 717
Glennallen, AK 99588
http://www.tazlinaglacier.com

This is a work of fiction. Names, characters, businesses, places, events and incidents are either the products of the author's imagination or used in a fictitious manner. Any resemblance to actual persons, living or dead, or actual events is purely coincidental.

Cover design by:
Andrei Bat via 99 designs
https://99designs.com/profiles/bandrei

Dedication to Frank Medina

Frank was my step dad. We rode a lot of fence in the high desert of Idaho together. I don't know where he found all the horses we broke, but I'll bet Satan was glad when he found out they were gone.

It was obvious that anyone who knew the country would not be in this end of the valley. They would know there was no way out. Besides that, why would there be so many men traveling together and why so far from any known road? They appeared to be following his tracks step for step. His rapidly pounding heart already knew the answer to his questions. This looked like a posse, or it might be vigilantes. Vigilantes wouldn't be asking many questions.

TABLE OF CONTENTS

Chapter 1

Yesterday's Gone

Talon of the Lakota Windcatcher people sat silent on the ground in the first light of day. He had sat there most of yesterday as well. The rising sun slowly crept across the South Dakota prairie and stretched the shadow of his mother's grave marker as far as it could reach before it began to shrink again.

He was a young man, not quite twenty years old. He was also a poor man. Struggle had been a way of life since his father had died ten years earlier.

That grave was on the other side of his mother's from where he sat. His mother, laid here just yesterday, was now sleeping with his father again, and for the most part, Talon was alone. Someone who knew his mother had carved words into the wood marker that read: "Here is the sleeping place of Mary Fall Wind of the Windcatcher people. If she had any thorns they were hidden among the roses."

Talon looked down at his well-worn moccasins and wondered what he should do. His mother had been the last of his personal family. He had an uncle and cousins, but of his own family, she was the last. The Windcatcher people were dwindling in number if one only counted the living. Talon counted them all. The dead, he believed, were only sleeping, or maybe they were in some other place, but he knew in his heart that they were not gone. They were still his people.

Now he was feeling very lost. The sun was lifting into the sky and he was feeling the need to move.

He had grown up in the fashion of the old-school way of the Lakota and still wore his buckskin clothes. Others of the reservation still used them a little, but most had gone to using the clothes of the white man.

He wished he could. He liked the cotton and wool better, but money was tight. His own clothes reminded him of the days of his father. He liked them also because they wore longer, but at the moment they had been wet by the moist night air and morning dew and made him feel cold.

He thought to go home to his mother's lodge. The cabin he had been born in had burned long ago, so the lodge had become home.

Maybe he would know who he was if he looked again at who he had been, but that was then and this was a new day. He had stayed in his mother's lodge the last night she was alive but had not gone back. He was sure it would feel more like her tomb than his home. Everywhere he let his eyes rest he would see her, so when he left he had taken all that he owned with him, and it wasn't much.

He had the clothes on his back, his knife, and his father's 45-70 rifle. It had one round of ammunition, which was old and might not fire. There was no reason to worry about that. He had never fired a gun and didn't expect that he could hit a river standing on a bridge. He also had the bow his uncle had made for him. Besides that and one silver dollar, all he had were memories of other days.

He knew he needed a plan, but all he could come up with sounded crazy. Still, the more he thought on it, the better it sounded. It involved a story he first had heard when he was a small boy. The medicine makers warned the people not to talk of it. There was fear that it would open doors in the other world and evil spirits might start visiting among the Lakota, spirits that might bring death or bad luck.

Talon first heard of it when he was very young and it talked of a time before his father was a child. The story told of a cabin in a far away place that belonged to his mother, now that his father had died. It was a cabin she would never have gone to possess, even if she thought she wanted to. He heard a much-polluted version of it again only a few nights before, by one of the young men he hung with.

4

They said that the cabin was made of stone and that it was in a land of tall mountains where animals of all kinds lived. There were said to be animals there he had never seen before. The story told that they were easy to catch and good to eat. It talked of rivers flowing with fresh clean water, deep and clear, a land where life was easy and quiet.

A cabin made of stone was not something Talon had ever seen and he wondered if it was from one stone like it had been carved, or if of many stones. No one seemed to know much of the details. He also wondered what kind of animals were there, and wished to see them. All he could find on the Reservation were rabbits and ground squirrels. Sage hens were around, but most of them had been eaten by then. The deer and antelope on the reservation were all but wiped out by the white settlers, and the buffalo had been gone for a long time. Some local ranchers kept a few to try to revive the herd, but they were privately owned. He had never eaten the meat.

The government sent cows to the Reservation. He liked beef, but he wished for the old way, to hunt like his father and all those before him.

No one seemed to know who had built the cabin in the first place, but that wasn't important. What was, is that according to the legend, people went into the cabin but they never came out. That was why the elders and the medicine men were so afraid to talk of it. He knew very little of the story, and what little he did know he could not be sure of. What he did know was someone who he could learn it from, if he could get him to tell.

Talon's uncle was called Simeon Red Earth. He was his father's brother. The cabin had once been his father's and now had fallen to him. He was certain that his uncle would know.

The sun was climbing and getting warm when Talon decided what he would do. His uncle had a lodge not far from his mother's. The cabin was Talon's now, and his uncle could not refuse him the story even if he wanted to.

Simeon was old. His lodge was old as well, but the canvas was still good and he didn't plan to need it much longer. Talon worried for his uncle. He didn't seem to have much life left in him and he had been all the father Talon could remember. He was young when his own father died.

Simeon seemed to be glad to see Talon and brought him in to sit and talk.

"You have come back from your Mother and Father now. What can you tell me you plan for tomorrow?" asked Simeon.

Talon sat by the edge of the fire spot, now growing cold. The light was dim and the air smelled of the good smell of smoke, as did the hair and clothes of his aging uncle.

Talon was not sure where he should begin. He worried that his uncle would not want to tell him what he needed to know. He was close to his uncle and knew that if he tried to soften the question too much his uncle might be insulted by the deception. It was best he decided, to cut to the chase.

"I have come," said Talon, "to talk of yesterday. Talk of tomorrow will come after. You are the last of my people and I respect you as much as I respect my life. Yet, when I think of my days so far I am reminded that a great secret has been kept from me since my beginning. Now I wish to know it and you are the only one who I know of to tell me.

"I am told of it in bits and pieces, but only in whispers. They say that my people own a cabin in a far away place, in a good land where there is game. That is all I can learn, except that it is called spirit house and feared by all who know of it. Still, it is mine now and I wish to know of it. Will you tell me, my uncle, what is this story?"

"I suspected you might want to know, and I can tell you, "said Simeon. "But know this much, it is not a place you should think of going. It is a very bad place. I know what your father told me of it, and all that his father told him. It is a bad place, but it is yours to know, and I am the one who must pass it on. Now I will tell you.

"There was a time long ago, in a land I have never seen, where a good people lived. A day came when they made themselves stronger and their hunting land bigger. It seemed easier than it should have been to take the land, and soon they learned why.

In the new land stood a cabin with stone walls. It was hidden in a small valley by where a clear river flowed. The walls of the valley were straight up and flat. They were made of the same stone of the cabin and very high on the side the cabin was on.

On the other side was a very steep hill with trees at first and rock higher up. The mountain, it was said, was trying to hide the cabin because it knew of the spirits there.

The people are called the Nez Perce, and they are in the land still. Not long after they found the cabin, evil spirits sent the white man's sickness, and death followed. Sickness was in every lodge, and they learned from a captive that the cabin was why.

"The captive told of how men in the past had gone into the cabin and lived there. He said that in the cabin was gold and that the men were happy there for a little time, but soon came the day when they went into the cabin and did not come out.

"What kind of a place is this, asked the people, where a man is taken in his sleep and not returned? We have brought to our people a great evil and now we, as did the other people, must be rid of it.

"Then they went to the people of our close neighbors the Cheyenne, and they tried to give the land with the cabin to them, but the Cheyenne were careful not to take it and the offer fell to the Lakota.

"The deal sounded good at first. If any far away people would take the cabin, and the spirits with it, perhaps the spirits would not travel to them, and the Nez Perce people would be freed of the evil. For this, the Nez Perce would give four strong horses and four good robes. The cabin then would not be theirs. The Nez Perce believed that as long as no one came to disturb the spirits, as they had done, they would be safe.

"Our people were the poorest of the nation and they took the deal. No one in our family ever went to the cabin. No one of us would take the chance that they might bring back spirits when they returned. Now you are asking to know and I have told you, but you must never go there Talon. It is evil. If you do you might disturb the spirits and if they come here, we might find death among us as well."

Talon had already decided he was going. It was all he had and this place called the reservation was, as he saw it, more about death than life already. Talon sat silent for a moment. He knew what he wanted, but he knew it would not go over well with his uncle. After a while, he decided to say what was in his heart.

"I will go," said Talon. "I will go and see this valley of good and live there. If the cabin seems bad I will not live in it, but I will live in the good land."

"You must not Talon. If you go there you will die as all those before you. It is easy to think you are different when you are young, as you are, but other men, strong men, were taken easily by spirits. Do you wish to die as they did?"

Talon realized what his uncle was saying might be true, but he was more afraid of life on the reservation than of spirits that might not even be real.

"If I stay here, what is there here for me? How can a boy become a man here now? All the ways of our fathers are gone, and we have put them into the ground with their bodies.

"Now we look back because there is no light to show us the future. We no longer go to war with the Crow or the Snake to take horses and captives. All our dance fires are cold and there is no way to prove a man. I will go to challenge the life I can not see. If I win, I will be a man. If not, I will die as a man, but either way, I will live free, and not a captive in this cage without bars where we are kept.

"If I stay here, I sleep among the memories of our fathers the way a man sleeps among the dead. A man who is neither dead nor alive, he can not go back, and he will not go forward. You must tell me how I can find this people called the Nez Perce. They will show me the way to the cabin if any of them remembers."

12

Simeon sat and stared at the ground, for what seemed a long time to Talon, and said nothing. Talon knew that his uncle held the pathway to tomorrow and that he needed to reason with what Talon had told him before he would say where it lay if he would.

After a while, Simeon picked up a little twig and dropped it into the fire pit. The fire was gone from the pit and it lay there unburned.

"I fear that what I am about to tell you will be as it is with this twig," he said. "Soon enough, the women will come, and without looking, will set the little fire that we cook with and the tiny stick will go unnoticed into the smoke and drift away. Still, I will tell you. I cannot hide from you what is yours to know.

"I will not try to stop you from going because I see your heart and it is strong, but if you disturb the spirits and death comes here I will say in my own heart that I have brought it in my telling.

"Nevertheless, I too will die a man, for your words have made me understand that we must both challenge tomorrow and live or die as men. Perhaps you are right that all we have left is the memories of our past now long dead."

For the next couple of hours, Simeon told Talon of where he should be able to find the people called the Nez Perce, who knew of the cabin. He drew a map, as well as he could, of the land to the west where he should look. He had been a long many days to the west, as a young man, but not as far as the place Talon would need to get to. Beyond there, he could only guess.

He told Talon that along his way he would find the white settlements, and not be well received. He would also find small towns that did not exist when he was last there, and many other things to be aware of.

He also told of the Black Foot people, who could be trusted to try to kill him if they got the chance. Then he told him of the amazing spotted horses of the Nez Perce. "That is how you will know them," he said. "All the horses are very much the same. They are strong and fast and have light colored rumps with dark spots on them. Not like any other you have seen."

Talon sat and listened. It was exciting to him, to see what lay ahead, and he was eager to start, but he knew that it would not be easy.

"It seems a long way," said Talon. "If I try to walk there, the winter will find me long before I find this place."

"Yes, it is long." Simeon said, "But maybe I have a plan for that. Come here again, when the sun is red and setting. I will talk to a friend of ours. He will want to see you, now that you are leaving anyway."

"I will come again," said Talon. Talon sat on the edge of a small draw and watched the sun sink slowly into the west. Shadow fell on the westward side of the little valley and sun reflected red in the tops of the trees tall enough to reach it. A ground squirrel suddenly moved up the hill on the other side of the draw from Talon and retreated into its hole.

Night was soon to fall and Talon could hear all

the familiar things he had heard from as far back as he could remember. Tiny frogs began to sing and crickets started their dance music.

It was the same as it had always been, but this time it seemed very different. This time seemed like the last time. It seemed like a farewell they were singing. The boy of yesterday was fading into the past, and the man to be would be in another place far away, and would never see or hear these things in this place again.

In one way, it saddened him. It seemed like all of his life had been about staying alive here, and being part of this place.

It was hard now to remember the days when he was young and all of life was a world to explore. The day had long passed since he had begun to feel as though he had discovered all there was to see here. The day he realized that, was the day he realized that this was a place of dying. What he remembered now was hard work and the constant fading away of his fathers who had come before him.

Red Cloud had been right. He had sued the White Man's government in their own courts and had won.

You can win, thought Talon, *but not here.*

The older he got, the harder it had become to want this place, where all he knew was working other people's horses and scratching the earth with his mother for whatever could be raised in the little patch of ground near her tipi.

Losing his mother had brought about another day now, and he knew he could never go back to any of the days before. Still, it seemed sad to turn his back and walk away.

The night would always be musical to him, and he knew he would miss some of the things that he had always known, *but so it is with all the earth* he told himself.

A night hawk cried in the sky above him and it was what made him rise to leave. This was goodbye.

The sun had dropped to below the horizon and the sky was darkening when Talon reached the little ridge that his uncle had set his lodge on. It was hidden in the pine, along the edge of a small canyon rim where small cedar trees grew among large stone. If you didn't know where to look for it, you would not find it easily. Talon had been there many times and knew the trail well.

A light wind was drifting through the trees, and it seemed good to be alive. Good to know that the morning would bring an entire life with it. No matter what that life might be, it would be far away from this place, where there seemed no life remained. Only the echoes of the past life, before the fire-water and sickness, came to his people.

He had no idea what his uncle was planning, but he knew his uncle, and he knew that if there was a way to help, his uncle would know how to do it.

When Talon entered the small clearing where his uncle's lodge stood, he saw that there were six horses tied in the trees behind it. Two of them were friends of his.

His uncle had company. Any other time he

would have turned and left. It was not good to intrude on another's company, but this time he had been invited, and he was glad. He was eager to hear of his uncle's plan.

Inside the lodge were voices of men talking and laughing. They all called out when they saw Talon as if a man, and not a boy, had entered the lodge. It felt good to Talon. It gave him confidence in himself to be treated like a man by the men he had always respected as his elders.

All of the men in the lodge were older men except for one, who was about Talon's age. His name was Fred Follows The Horses. He was the son of Falling Water. Falling Water had a lot of horses and Talon had broke a few of them so that he could sell them. Selling horses had become difficult and grass was harder to find every year, it seemed.

Talon and Fred were friends, and whenever he was needed to help with the horses, Talon made sure to be there. He had learned many things working for Falling Water with Fred and had never asked for any pay. He knew that no one had much money and he liked the work. He liked the horses too, even the mean ones.

Talon had recognized one of the horses tied in the trees. It was a tall powerful gelding that Falling Water had castrated as a three-year-old. It was late in life to be cut, but the horses were gaining in number too fast and needed to be slowed. The horse had been a good stud and was now a proud cut, who still tried to ride the mares like he refused to recognize his new position in the way of things.

He was a long-legged horse and fast. He was painted but had normal brown eyes. Some of the paints had one glass eye. It made them look strange to Talon. He was glad this one didn't. Talon liked him and had ridden him anytime he got the chance. The horse recognized Talon when he saw him. He tossed his head and snorted a little. It made Talon smile. Next to the big horse was another horse not quite as big, but stout. It was a mare with a blaze face and four matching stockings. Talon thought he knew her as well. If he was right, she was good to ride or pack.

Both horses had been mustangs in the first years of their life and were smart, good animals. Talon wondered who had ridden them in. The gelding had a homemade bit and head rig and there were blankets on him for a saddle. Now in the lodge, he wondered even more. Six horses were tied outside but only five men were in the lodge and one of them was his uncle.

"Talon," Simeon called out. "Sit down. We have waited for you."

Some of the men had been drinking a little, and Talon could smell it in the lodge. Talon waved respectfully at Falling Water and the other men and sat near the lodge door to listen.

"I have asked Falling Water here to talk of horses for you to ride for your long travel."

Talon noticed that Simeon had not mentioned the Spirit house and thought it wise to avoid it himself. Falling Water was sitting next to Simeon.

"Where will you go?" asked Falling Water. "You are among us, and we will miss you if you go. I have talked a little with Simeon and I understand that you wish to prove yourself. It did not surprise me to learn that you have chosen to chase tomorrow.

"Fred also is feeling a little fire in his blood, and may follow you, but only if he knows where you went. It is hard to track the tiny spiders who drift on their out-stretched web on the wind. Even harder if he plans to take a herd of horses with him."

All the men in the lodge laughed and drank a little more.

"Simeon tells me only that you will wander far away. Do you have a place in mind?"

Talon thought for a moment and was careful how he answered.

"Who can see tomorrow?" he said. "I plan to find a plan as I go."

"Then you will send for me." said Fred, and the lodge filled with laughter again.

It was a good time and everyone was happy.

Talon had never sat among the older men before and he knew it would make leaving even harder. He also knew that this is how the drinking got its hold on men and made fools of them. He had never seen Falling Water or Fred drink before and they were far from drunk now, but that was now. Fire-water, Talon had observed, was a sly, cowardly enemy that slipped into the lodges unnoticed and brought death through the door with it.

"Before you got here," said Falling Water, "We were talking of the far away places you might go.

"I remembered Simeon went once, long ago, with Red Cloud to the place of the great father in the land called Washington. You were the size of a puppy in those days and often sounded like one."

Everyone laughed again. Even Talon could not resist the fun of it. He had not known that his uncle had gone anywhere with Red Cloud and especially not Washington.

"To Washington, with Red Cloud! How old were you uncle? You never told me. What did you do in the white man's counsel lodge?" Simeon didn't seem like he wanted to be in the spotlight. He looked at the pipe in his lap to think of what to say and for a moment was silent.

"I learned new things," said Simeon."

A small breeze moved up the little valley and for a moment the lodge smoke gathered in the top of the lodge, then puffed out through the smoke hole again.

"I remember you went," said Falling Water. "And I remember you came again, but you never said what other things you saw there and I never asked. What other things did you see there?"

Simeon looked up from his lap and smiled at his guests. It was a smile Talon had seen before. It usually meant he was up to something.

"Red Cloud was very old." He said." I went to be with him when he talked to the white chiefs of matters concerning his people. What I remember most was that I looked around and said 'Hoy' a lot, so that everyone knew I agreed with Red Cloud."

Everyone laughed at that.

"What did you agree about?" asked Fred.

"You are young," said Simeon. "Later you will learn to trust your elders. It's much easier than listening."

Then everyone really laughed, even Simeon.

"Tell me what you learned," said Falling Water. "You must have learned some new thing you never told."

"There is not much. I remember the talk in the great fathers' lodge," said Simeon. "It seemed to pass like clouds without rain. It was in the streets that I remember the most. There were many shops and people were everywhere. All the buildings were different colors and all the women wore fancy clothes. It was a lot to see.

"I will tell you one good thing I saw, in a loud place where men gambled with cards and tricks and won or lost many things. One man was especially good. He had a great trick and he won when he used it."

"A trick," said Falling Water. It was easy to see

that he was instantly interested. A new trick might be very interesting.

"Show me the new trick you have kept all this time to yourself."

"It is a trick to use when you are gambling, "said Simeon. You need to have something to gamble with, something to win or lose. I will show you the trick. If I win, will you agree to give Talon the two horses you brought with you?"

Talon's heart leaped in his chest. The gelding he had long respected and loved! So this is why the extra horses were tied outside. The thought of owning even a mean horse was a dream that he had not dared dream could come true. To own the proud cut and the mare would be more to him than gold to the white man.

What Talon could not know was that Falling Water had set in his heart to give the horses to Talon when he brought them. He had come to love Talon like a son over the long years of his boyhood.

When Talon's father died, Simeon and Falling

Water had taken up raising him. It was their influence that made him who he was, more than even he knew. Learning a new trick would make it all the more fun.

"Here is the trick I learned," said Simeon, "and here is my gambling deal. I wish to trade with Falling Water for two horses. This is what I offer."

Talon had in his hair three tail feathers of an eagle. They were tied in with strands of the hair of a horse's mane. Simeon slipped his knife from his belt and cut the feathers loose. Then he laid them on the ground in front of Falling Water. Falling Water stared for a moment at the feathers and then he laughed.

"How can you trade three feathers for two horses?" He asked, amused.

"It is the trick," said Simeon. "You see three feathers but there are really four of them."

Falling Water looked more serious now as he stared at the feathers. Everyone was looking at them now, and the lodge was silent while they waited to see what Simeon's trick might be.

"Four," said Falling Water. "Not four. Only three. Did you forget how to count in Washington? This won't be much of a trick if it can't even fool a half-drunk Indian."

The whole lodge laughed again.

"Look more closely," said Simeon. "Be very careful so no one will laugh at you later."

Falling Water carefully separated the feathers to be sure one more was not hidden behind the others. There were only three.

"So this is a trick of counting," he said.

"No," said Simeon, "no trick with counting. You can see them on the ground. Four, no trick. How can you not see them? In front of you are four feathers."

Falling Water looked at them again and laughed. Then he separated them again with his fingers and began to wonder what Simeon was up to. One of the other men leaned over and touched the feathers with his fingers. He looked at Falling Water and laughed a little also. No one was eager to get involved until they had seen what kind of trick Simeon was playing.

"I am old but I'm not crazy yet," said Falling Water. "Here in front of me lay three feathers and they are to trade for two horses, so now I am interested in how this is to be done."

"Here is mystery," said Simeon. "I have put down four feathers and I have tricked my friends into thinking I have only offered three.

"Falling Water is saying to me he has counted all the feathers and finds only three. I am also able to count and I will not touch the feathers to change any of them. I will not count twice or try to use any trick about the number of them.

"I am saying there are four feathers only because that is how many there are. With no disrespect for my friends, I am amazed that men of your age cannot see all the feathers. To me, it is easy to see and I will not change my mind.

"Here is the problem then. Falling water says three, and I say four. We cannot both be right. So count again Falling Water, and be very careful to be sure. I say three, and you say four. Are you sure of this thing?"

Falling Water almost said yes but suddenly realized what Simeon had just said.

"Not four," said Falling Water, sounding a little confused. "You said three, no I mean four. You said four, not three."

He was about to laugh again, his head spinning a little.

"Okay," said Simeon. "Four. I did say four because there are four. You say there are three. I say there are four. If I am wrong will you give Talon the horses?"

Falling Water laughed again and looked at the feathers.

"Yes," he said, a little uncertain.

He wasn't sure what Simeon was thinking, and he knew there was a trick hidden someplace in his words, but he couldn't find it.

"Good" yelled Simeon. "The horses are yours Talon. I am wrong."

Falling Water was stunned for an instant and instantly replayed the last words Simeon had used. When he realized what had been done, he roared with laughter, as did all the lodge. Talon smiled. In fact, he smiled so hard he thought his face might crack, and then he laughed at the great trick. Washington, it seemed, was good for something after all.

Talon could feel a new life growing out of the ashes of the old one. The lodge was filled with laughter and the night was clear and good. Best of all, he now had horses.

He had often dreamed of having horses of his own. Now not only did he have horses, he had horses he knew and trusted.

The gelding was more powerful than other horses, and faster. Both horses were mustang. That meant they would find their own way through the trees and brush, even at a dead run. The American horses that came with the white man were good horses, but if you rode them hard they would fall into trouble. They would run through prairie dog towns, where the holes would cause them to fall and break their legs. They wouldn't find the best path through the brush either.

The gelding needed a good rider with strong legs. If he decided to make a hard turn at a run he would run out from under a man who was not prepared for how fast he moved. He was the perfect horse for Talon. The mare was not as fast as the gelding, and she was more than Talon needed for a packhorse. At this point in his life, all he owned he could wrap up in his bedroll and tie onto the gelding behind him.

Talon knew that Simeon was wise about such things so he didn't question why he had asked for both horses. He felt very rich to have them and eager to start his ride north. He had begun to dream of what it must look like in the new land. He thought of what he might find along his way on his long journey, and somewhere in his dreaming and the laughter he slept.

Chapter 2

The Edge of Tomorrow

Morning birds woke him a little before the sun opened its bright eye to stare at the earth below. Talon sat up and tried to see in the dark lodge. The light was just moving down from the smoke hole, and he could see faces still sleeping all around him. He looked at them for a long while. It was an image he wanted to keep always. These were men he loved as much as he loved the free wind and the horses. These were faces he might never see again in this life, and he knew they were faces of men who loved him.

He was still looking at the sleeping men when he realized he could not see Simeon in the lodge. *He must be outside,* thought Talon and slipped out of the door flap without a sound.

Outside the air was more fresh and cool. Talon found Simeon coming from the direction of some of the other lodges not far away. He was holding something in his arms. It was about all he could carry. He went behind the lodge, where the horses were, and laid it down in a pile with other things he had already put there. Talon followed him to where he was working to see what he was up so early doing.

In the pile were many useful things, among which were a coffee pot, a small boiling pot, rope, and food. Some of it was meat. Other things were there like coffee and greens from the trading post. More things were buried in the little pile and below them was an English-style pack saddle and canvas bags called panniers, designed to be carried on a cross-tree saddle.

"Did you raid the whole village?" asked Talon.

Simeon smiled. "These are from your neighbors, Talon. Some gave a little, some a little more. Maybe they still love you or, maybe they just want to get rid of you."

Both men laughed a little. Talon stared at the pile of goods on the ground beside the mare, almost in disbelief. He had not thought of what he would need for the trip. He only knew what he had, and planned on getting the rest as best he could.

In this pile were things he would not have realized he needed until he was found to be without them. *My neighbors,* thought Talon. He had not thought of them as neighbors, but only as the people who were always there. They didn't seem to much more than notice him when he saw them. Now he saw them in a very different light.

Simeon had known his heart from talking to him and watching him grow ever more restless with the reservation. It was not hard for him to see that Talon was moved in his spirit.

"Have you noticed these trees?" asked Simeon. "Do you see how some of the limbs always die first? I wonder if they are just older, or maybe more tired from all the winters. Whichever it is, I have seen that they do not affect the rest of the tree. It stands tall and strong as ever."

Talon knew what Simeon was saying. He realized that he had been too hard on his people in his heart. In spite of all who had fallen to the fire-water, or had lost their heart for the fight, they were still very good people. He also realized how much he loved them and how much they loved him. The pile was not a gift to make him stay; it was a gift to help him go.

These were still his people, and no matter what else, they were all one blood. Lakota blood. It made him very proud to be one with such a strong people.

"Time," said Simeon, "has not swept our people away. We have moved many times. Not always because we chose to. We came here from the other side of the great river. This is only our most recent place, not our last.

"We have pushed others off the land and been pushed from our own. Still, we survive and stay strong. One day all men will know the great power of the Lakota blood and realize how strong we are. Today looks bad, and I am glad you are pushed in your spirit to prove your heart. It is the way of our people and not many keep it now. I see that it is good, but go with a good heart for your people and come again to us when you can."

Talon stood for a moment and thought of the gifts of his people. He hoped that somehow he would come again, but he knew he must go. He put out his hand and Simeon took it in his own.

"You are wise," said Talon. "My heart is good for my people."

Nothing more was said as Simeon helped Talon saddle the pack mare and load the panniers. The light of day had not been long in the sky when Talon leaped to the top of the gelding. He took one last look at his uncle and turned to leave. Falling Water came out of the lodge as Talon was riding past, and Talon waved and smiled. Falling Water waved and smiled back.

The sky was promising a warm day, and yet Talon's heart was heavy. For a time he rode on and thought of all he had known of the land he was leaving and the people that lived there. Soon, however, that sadness of farewell gave way to the spirit of youth and the weight he had been carrying lifted. The farthest, most western edge of the reservation came and went and the horses felt strong and eager. The past was for the moment behind him and the day was his.

Chapter 3

The Clantons

The land was broken and created little valleys that seemed to go nowhere. Following them was time-consuming and made it necessary to wander off course too much. It also meant he needed to climb up one side of a ridge, only to climb down the other. The answer Talon discovered was to remain on the tops and work the ridges. He found that if he looked ahead far enough he could see where to cut across and where he could ride the ridges looking into the little valleys. Where one ridge ended he could easily cross a little valley to where another started.

It was slow going at first but in the course of time got easier. Little meadows of grass with islands of trees spotted the land. Passing from one little grassland to the next was only a matter of riding around the little islands.

The day passed, and then another, and still others. The land gradually changed a little every day and in a couple weeks became flatter. He also noticed that on occasion he found a tree he had not noticed before.

One in particular was some sort of pine, much taller than any other he had seen. The bark was rougher as well. He began to notice other things that were not the same as well. Grouse he had not noticed on the reservation were plentiful. He had eaten a few of them and liked the meat.

So far, this new life was good and every day brought a new excitement with it. He rode through the trees and grass looking ahead as if to see something new on every meadow. The paint's ears picked up any time a deer or coyote moved in the distance.

It caught Talon's attention every time and caused him to stop and look until he too saw what the horse had seen.

He wished he had a dog as well. They were better at smelling than horses and could find snakes easier. A few times he had encountered fences. Not many, but enough. They caused him to need to follow them until he could ride past. Inside the fences were the livestock of settlers. Talon realized why they needed the fences but he didn't like finding them.

They were a relatively new addition to the plains and not everyone liked them, especially a lot of the larger ranchers. They hated them because they blocked open range. That was the reason the small settlers liked them. They kept other people's stock from using up the grass they needed for their own. There had been local wars over the fences and men had died fighting for the right to keep what they had.

Talon wasn't fond of the fences himself. They were made of wire that was hard to see in the dark and he worried about riding into one in the night. Also, they made travel hard and seemed rude. Like a statement that said "Stay out. We don't like you, go away." He hoped that all the people were not as rude as the fences seemed to be.

A few hours after Talon had broke camp one morning he came onto one of the fences and rode along it to its end. Where the fence ended, the wire lay on the ground just beyond where it had been nailed to the last post. The fence was not finished. Talon wondered how far it would go to its end and rode past it in the direction he had been headed when he found it.

He was thinking of how much work it must be to do such things when a bullet blew past within inches of his head and slammed into a tree six feet behind him. He heard the roar of the rifle as he hit the ground and rolled behind a pine tree. He had been caught totally off guard and tried to gather his thoughts while he looked for the origin of the bullet.

The 45-70 was on the mare and she had spooked

and run with the gelding for a short way down the trail. The rifle shot had come from close by and that was all that Talon knew. He remained on the ground behind the tree and lay motionless.

"Now I know you ain't hit," someone yelled from a few yards away. "You might as well stand up. If I wanted you dead you would be."

The sound of his voice gave Talon a direction and when he looked he saw what he was looking for. The fence was on a small ridge and a draw ran from there to a little valley some distance below. He could see a man's head at about ground level. He appeared to be standing in the draw.

Talon kicked himself for being caught by surprise. Had he been looking, or even watching the paint's ears, he would have seen him before. Had he been expecting company, he told himself, he would have been looking. It was not a mistake he planned to make ever again. That is if he ever got the chance.

He looked around for a way out, but where he was afforded no good escape. The shooter must have been watching him for some time and chose where to start trouble. Still, Talon reasoned, he could have killed me like he said.

"Why are you shooting at me?" Talon yelled back.

"You're on private land, Injun."

Talon could hardly believe his ears. Many whites had crossed the reservation and were not even noticed, much less shot at.

"I didn't know you shoot people who ride on your land," said Talon." Have you killed any of your neighbors yet?"

"Wasn't trying to kill ya. Just a warnin. You got no business here. This here is private land."

Talon had been treated poorly by whites before and not only by them but even some of the other tribes that traded at the trading post back home. He had never been shot at. He found it humiliating but was grateful the shooter only meant to scare him and not kill. He wasn't sure what he should do. He had no way to defend himself. His bow and his rifle were not with him and he didn't know what he would do if they had been. He looked for his horses and saw them about thirty yards away down the trail he had been following.

They were too far away to reach easily, so he did the only thing he could think of and stood up. It gave him a better view of the shooter. He had lowered the rifle and was looking at Talon from under the limbs of a small cedar, standing in the lower elevation the little draw provided.

"I'm only riding through. I never expected it to be such a problem. Tell me where your line is and I will go around."

The shooter began moving up through the little draw to the ridge where Talon was. When he did, Talon discovered he was sitting on a horse. The draw was deeper than it looked and Talon realized that the shooter was working on the fence when he had arrived and made a dive for his horse and the protection of the little draw.

He acts like a hunted man, thought Talon.

"Not looking to hurt anyone, said Talon.

"Headed north, just riding through."

The shooter looked to be a man in his early for-
ties, and average build. He seemed uneasy, even
though he had full control of the situation — he
had the gun. He first carefully studied Talon from
his heels up and then looked around like he might
find someone else hidden in the trees, who had
come with him.

"Where you from?" He wanted to know as he
kept looking around. His voice was not that of a
friendly person. Talon wasn't sure how far he had
ridden since home. The trip had been fun and he
had wandered like a coyote from one nice looking
meadow and water hole to the next.

Many days had passed, and the weather had
been good for travel. He had only the sun and stars
to choose his direction with, and a lot of his time
had been spent just drifting along. Simeon had giv-
en him a map of the area he remembered, drawn
on a small piece of doeskin with charcoal, but it
was too general to be much use. He decided to tell

what he did know and hope the shooter would not think him a fool.

"From South Dakota," he said, hoping he was not still in South Dakota.

The gelding had gotten over his surprise and walked back up the trail to where Talon was standing. The mare was with him. The shooter looked over Talon's horses with the same careful study he had afforded Talon.

"You got a name, Injun?"

"Name's Talon."

The shooter was more than a little nervous and the last thing Talon wanted was to give him reason to feel more so. He was still the only one with a gun.

"Not to seem pushy," said Talon, "but what do people call you... I mean the ones that like you?"

"Name's Ed Clanton. Don't matter if they like me or not. Believe it or not, most folks that know me like me just fine."

You must not shoot at them much, thought Talon.

"The one that don't like me is one of my

neighbors. Seems they have a lot more than I got and that ain't enough. They want what little grass I got on top of what they got. So I started putting up this here fence. They don't like my fence and keep making threats bout how they plan to put a stop to it even if it means killing me. I don't think they're bluffing.

"They've already run off other people like me. They call us squatters. Must be pretty easy to forget when they were startin' out. Anyway, it don't do much for a man's confidence towards strangers, if you get my meaning."

Talon got his meaning without any trouble. Now he understood why Ed Clanton had shot at him. It made him a little more at ease. The two men stood for a moment and studied one another. Talon decided he had seen enough and wanted to be on his way.

"If you got no problem with it," said Talon "I'll get back on my horse and just keep riding. You look like you got trouble enough and I got a long way to go."

Talon leaped back onto the back of the gelding and started back the way he was going when

Clanton's bullet had stopped him. He hoped that Ed wasn't as mean spirited as he seemed. *Must have caught him off guard as well,* he thought. The humiliation of being shot at and having to hit the ground still irritated him but he decided he would live and kept riding.

"Well if you're headed north," said Ed, "you should know there ain't good water for the next fifteen miles or so. Talon stopped and looked back at Ed. That was not good news. He had not found water since morning and was hoping to find some soon.

"No water?" said Talon

"Well none I know of," Ed said. He had decided that Talon wasn't any threat, and felt a little more comfortable with him.

"I got a stock tank down at the house if you want to water your horses before you leave. Just in the way of being neighborly and all."

Talon figured it was as close to an apology as he would get or maybe as much as he should expect. Hanging around with Ed didn't hold much appeal to Talon but if he was right about the water, there was only one thing he could do.

"That would be good," said Talon. "How do I find it?"

Ed looked around at the fence and then back to Talon. He thought of just telling him to follow the ridge to the meadow but remembered his wife and daughter. They would not be expecting strangers, especially Indian strangers.

"I can take you." He said.

He turned his horse downhill and rode out ahead of Talon.

Ed kept a watchful eye on Talon the whole way down the winding little path that wandered through the trees to the cabin. Half an hour later they left the thick of the trees and entered an open meadow. From there Talon could see the cabin and corrals. Near the cabin stood a barn and there was also a root cellar dug into the bank and a hen house not far on the other side of the cabin.

As the two men approached, a young woman

hurried from the hen house with her skirt tail bundled full of eggs. Long blond hair drifted in the breeze as she made her way to the cabin and closed the door behind her.

The stock tank was in front of the barn. Half of it was on the other side of the corral fence where Ed had a couple horses. Talon noticed they looked young and looked American bred. They were barefooted and their manes and tails were tangled. He had seen a lot of horses that looked like them on the reservation. They looked like they had just been brought in from the range.

He brought his own horses to a halt at the long wooden tank. The water inside was clean, clear and cold. It spilled in from a pipe at the end that never stopped running. At the other end of the trough was a "v" cut into it that let the water out. From there it watered the meadow as far as it could before returning to the earth again. Ed had trapped a small spring someplace up on the surrounding hills and piped it down to the cabin. Gravity gave it enough pressure to supply the cabin and barn with constant fresh water. *Good idea,* thought Talon. He found his cup in the pack and held it under the running water and drank from the cold sweet water of the spring as he studied the horses in the corral.

"What do ya make of em?" asked Ed. "Got em at auction a couple months ago. Don't usually keep mares around, but couldn't pass em by. Got em for bout nothin. Never been rode though. Still need broke. All they're good for right now is burning hay. You any good at breakin horses? Asked Ed.

"Broke both mine," said Talon. "I like most horses more than I do most people." He was deliberately looking at Ed as he spoke.

Ed chuckled. "I got that," he said.

He seemed a little more at ease now that they were at the cabin. Even there, he was still looking around as if someone might be watching him. It made him look like a man guilty of something to Talon.

This war Ed was in was a white man problem. It looked to Talon like this could be a good part of the country to avoid. Someone could end up dead, especially someone like him. It seemed to him that the white men found it easier to overlook a dead Indian than a white man. It kept him watchful of his words and left him wandering in shadow when he could.

Being Lakota, if they knew he was, would help him in a scrape with the law. They were a very large nation, even though a lot of them had been killed in the wars of the past. That had been a long time ago, and now the Lakota were stronger in number. Not at all like they once had been, but enough that trouble with them was avoided whenever possible.

The chance of a new war happening was still very real. War with a smaller nation would be less a threat than with the Sioux.

Besides that, Red Cloud had showed them how to fight in the white man's court if they chose to. The chief counsel of the people would not hesitate to pull the white man's law before one of their own judges. It would be a battle that would be long and hard.

Then there was the possibility of a ground war and under the right circumstances, both could happen. The white man believed that the nation was still stronger than Talon believed it to be. He wondered how strong they were and hoped that he would never need to know.

The problem was that most white men wouldn't know a Sioux apart from any other nation. It was getting harder to tell even for the Lakota. The people were not using traditional colors and lifestyle any longer and one Indian looked a lot like the next to the average person. In the end, none of that mattered to Talon. He planned to avoid any more trouble and this looked like trouble to him.

Ed lived like a hunted man. Talon was glad it wasn't him. The sooner he could water his horses and hit the trail the better. His experience with the white men at the agency had not left him trusting them. Ed Clanton hadn't done anything to improve on that.

"Thanks for the water," Talon said.

He stepped to the side of the paint and was

ready to leap onto his back when he caught movement from the corner of his eye.

Janice Clanton had come out onto the porch. The two men hadn't noticed her. She was Ed's wife. She was slight of build and had blond hair tied in a bun on the top of her head. She was smiling. *What,* thought Talon, *no gun?*

He was glad to see the smile but it seemed odd to him. He was Indian. That should be a concern to a white woman. Most of all the white women who had ever looked at him seemed upset or afraid. None of them were smiling.

"Ed," she called out cheerfully, "you brought company and never said. I'll set another plate for lunch. It will be ready in about ten minutes."

She stepped back into the house before either man could respond. Talon looked at Ed a little surprised. Ed looked a little surprised himself.

"I don't need to stay," said Talon. "I need to go."

Ed pulled a watch from his pocket and checked the time. It seemed a little early for lunch but he was already at the cabin, and by the time he got back to the fence it would be time to turn around and return to the cabin. The last thing he would have expected Janice to do was to offer a stranger, especially an Indian, a meal.

Nevertheless, it looked like she was in motion. That was a hard train to stop, and Ed knew it. Any other woman, thought Ed, would have run to the back of the cabin and waited for a stranger to leave, especially an Indian. Ed didn't hate Indians. He just didn't like them. She knows how it is with these Indians. I know she knows, thought Ed, and yet, she invited this one to dinner. Sometimes he wondered if maybe she just didn't like him.

So, thought Ed, *she wants it that way, does she? Well, two can play at that game.* All of a sudden, he decided that he did like Indians. The more they smelled like the trail the better. He hoped that she was expecting him to send Talon away even though she had invited him to eat. *Surprise, surprise*, thought Ed.

"Well you can spare a little time to eat can't ya?" Ed said. "Janice went to all the trouble of setting you a plate and all. She might take it for an insult if you leave now."

The look on Ed's face was the most pleasant Talon had seen all morning. It made him start to feel the way Ed had been looking all morning. Like something bad was about to happen. He really didn't want to stay. It was that "happy" look that Ed suddenly had on his face that made him suspicious. Don't be silly, he told himself. Just eat and get out as soon as possible. Besides that, he couldn't think of any good excuse to go without causing hard feelings.

"Just for a little while," Talon said.

When the men entered the cabin, the table was set with a thin linen cloth under a few dishes of different kinds of food, meat, and vegetables mostly, and a loaf of fresh bread.

The cabin was clean and the food smelled good. Especially the bread; it had just been taken from the oven. The clean, kept look of the cabin and table made Talon feel out of place. He was used to open fire and bare dirt. He suddenly remembered how much difference there was between his lifestyle and the one he was looking at.

He wondered if he smelled bad to the woman. His buckskins had not been washed in over a year. He didn't need them to be all that clean. Now he worried he might be a little offensive to these people of the more delicate type.

He also wondered how you should go about eating at a white man's table. He had never done that. Were there rules? He decided to wait and see how Ed did things and follow his lead.

Everything in the cabin looked scrubbed, even the floor. The only wood stove was the cook stove. It stood against the wall not far from the front door. Just on the other side of that was a comfortable-looking chair. Beyond the chair, was an open door that entered another smaller room. It looked like it could be a sleeping room. It had a door that was closed but the floor was worn in front of it like a well-worn path that led to that door. There was also a loft. It looked like the sleeping place for their daughter.

The cabin was larger than the ones that some of the people on the reservation had, and the ceiling was higher. It had one large log beam that ran the full length of the main room.

There were not many windows. One in the far end of the room, a large one, let light in onto a long work table. Built into the table was a machine for sewing. New clothes hung along the wall on a long pole. They appeared to be well-made and were hung on wooden hangers. A piece of linen a couple feet wide had been laid over the top of them to keep dust off. On the floor, there were bolts of colorful cloth, stacked or standing on end, all over that part of the room.

Janice motioned Talon to a chair on the side of the table near the end. Ed sat down next to him, on the opposite end from Janice. Talon waited to see what would happen next. Ed bowed his head and folded his hands. Talon had seen this at the mission so he bowed his also. Soon the rest of the family did the same. Once the prayer was over, Ed picked up one of the dishes. He took some food and handed it to Talon. Talon did the same. He wasn't sure how much he should take. He looked over at Ed's plate and took about the same amount. The bowls passed one at a time until they all had been sent around the table. How organized it all seemed. It made Talon feel a little silly.

In his world, you normally had only one pot and you took what you needed when you chose to do it. The food had passed, when the conversation started. Talon liked the colorful cloth and was looking at each bolt and shirt one at a time. He had never seen so much nice cloth in his life. He decided that Ed and Janice must be a lot richer than he first thought.

Janice noticed Talon was looking at the machine and cloth in the opposite end of the room.

"Do you like it?" Janice asked." I just got it. It's a singer treadle. It's much faster and easier than hand work."

"It's nice," said Talon.

He wasn't sure what else to say. He didn't want to tell her he wouldn't know it from any other. He had only seen a couple such machines in his life.

"I make clothes," Janice said. "I sell them when I can. Cotton and wool mostly, not much like your buckskins."

She didn't mean to sound impolite but was trying to say she could smell smoke and horse from across the room, without saying it. Talon caught the implication. He looked down at his sleeves and realized how out of place he must seem at such a clean, neatly covered table. He wished he could take his food outside to eat it, but that he realized, was not an option.

Ed was making more noise with his food than Talon could imagine a starving wolf might.

"It's his clothes," He blurted out with his mouth full of food.

Janice smiled and looked a little embarrassed. It made Talon blush a little.

"I like wool and cotton," Talon said. "I never had

any to wear but I have seen it in other places."

He tried not to mention the reservation for fear that they might think he was on the run for something. Most of the time these days, if an Indian left the reservation he was in some kind of trouble and couldn't be trusted. Trouble had taken on a whole new meaning in the land of the Lakota. What was once small battles between nations or families, was now punished. It was partly why Talon had chosen to leave in the first place. The white man's law would have brave men staying in the care of the women, never to become men.

"Of course he likes good clothes better, Janice." Ed interrupted," his voice as arrogant as usual.

He had pushed some of his food off his plate onto the tablecloth with a piece of bread as if it was an accident. Janice stared at it as it soaked through the cloth and left a bit of stain. Talon noticed it too. He looked at Janice, then away. She looked ready to blow.

The table went silent like things were about to

get interesting, but nothing happened. When she had gathered herself, Janice lifted her chin a little, took a deep breath, and smiled at Talon. *I need to go,* thought Talon. *I really need to go.*

Ed broke the silence. He was talking with his mouth full of food again, and it made a rude smacking noise as he tried to arrange it to talk.

"He ain't got the money to buy boots, much less decent clothes," he said. "You're making the man feel like a beggar."

Well, thought Talon, *at least he thinks of me as a man.* Janice turned red from her blouse to the top of her forehead. She gritted her teeth and looked as if she might bust into flame any second. The table went silent, and Talon hurried to finish his food so he could leave.

Ed's daughter Lacey sat in silence trying to hide behind her long blond hair. It was down, not in the bun she had before on the back of her head. She was a thin girl with pale skin like her mother. She seemed too shy for her own good and had sat in silence, not even asking for food to be passed. It was a bit of a surprise when she spoke.

"So," she said, as cheerful as she could make it sound, "I like your horses Mr. Talon. I haven't seen many other painted horses before. I have seen Ponies like that, but yours is much larger than they were. Where did you ever find such a fine animal?"

She was obviously trying to steer the conversation away from the silent rumble in the chair next to her. She knew her mother better than her father seemed to and was hoping to avoid another clash of the Titans like she had recently read about in school.

"They're mustangs," said Talon, between bites. He was grateful for the temporary reprieve. Almost finished, He told himself. He would have said more but Janice had taken the floor with the force of a storm.

"Mustang," she said. "How nice. Did you break them yourself?"

"Yes, ma'am."

"Imagine that," She said. "Did you hear that, Ed? He broke them himself. We have a couple horses that need broke. Perhaps we could work something out with you. How about you break our horses and I will make you a nice set of wool clothes."

Talon would have loved to have leapt from his chair and made a run for the door, but before he could move Ed raised his hand in what appeared a protest. He was instantly shot down by Janice, who obviously was not going to let him.

"I think that's a fine idea don't you Ed."

The tone she used could have frozen meat.

Ed suddenly looked up from his plate, like what she said surprised him. He looked at Janice, who knew what he must be thinking, and she smiled a sweet little smile at him.

Ed knew he could break the horses himself, but then he also knew Janice. He was trying to irritate her. It looked like it was going to be a game going in, but he must have overshot the line. Should have seen it coming, he told himself.

The bite in her voice told everyone within earshot that she had decided. Ed got the message loud and clear. He had her hot under the collar and was going to pay. It was too public for debate and Janice knew she had him. In short, she was going to make Talon a set of clothes and Ed was going to pay for the materials if he liked it or not. She almost laughed at the look on Ed's face when she said it. He looked at Janice and then at Talon. He had a suspicion that there might be more to this whole morning than could be seen, but couldn't put a handle on it. Maybe she wasn't looking for a fight. Well anyway, too late now.

"Sure, why not?" said Ed.

He had been here before and knew that things normally get worse the further he went. At this point, he decided, it was better to cut his losses and get back to his fence. Might just as well get something out of it, he decided. Better than feeding him for free.

Talon sat in amazement at what had just happened. They had made a decision about him, without so much as looking in his direction.

Unbelievable, thought Talon, *and all his neighbor wants to do is shoot him.*

He wanted to run for the door and ride hard and fast. The first problem with that plan was that he really wanted, and needed, the clothes. The next thing that he thought of was that breaking a couple horses for a full change of clothes was the equivalent of giving him the clothes for nothing. He loved horses and could work two at a time easy. No problem. The problem was that he also knew that Ed could do the work himself, and he had seen the attempt Ed had made at protest. That thought, for whatever reason, brought on another.

He suddenly remembered the rifle shot that brought him out of his saddle earlier that day. *So that's why she didn't come out with a gun,* thought Talon, *she don't need one.*

Talon glanced over at Ed. He was staring into his empty plate and looking a little whipped. He looked up when he realized Talon was looking at him. Talon smiled. The table had gone silent again and this time it was Talon who broke the silence. He could hardly believe his good fortune.

"Well," he said, standing up, "I guess I should make camp somewhere close. Is there anyplace you would prefer I stay?"

"Nonsense," said Janice. Ed's eyes widened. Dear God, he thought, she's not going to put him in the house I hope.

Ed wasn't evil, he just thought of Indians as a lesser people. A people, who as far as he knew, were not clean or civilized and could not be trusted. Janice cared little about who or what they were. She liked how Talon looked and could sense a sort of manner-ly way about him that she hoped to somehow cul-ture. She also liked the young muscular look of his trail-groomed body.

She looked over at Ed and could see that he was in a panic. It amused her. She knew Ed, and she knew she had him on the edge of his chair, and why. In truth, she would have had Talon in the house, but he would have a lot more privacy outside. Besides that, she was afraid of how it would look. *Anyway*, she told herself, *we have more suitable quarters, and Ed has gone about as far as he is going, without all out war.*

At that, she finished her original thought. "You can stay in the room we used as a house while we built this one," she said smiling. "You will find it on the east side of the barn."

That was good news to Talon, who suddenly realized that he could use a break from the trail. Ed stood up also and left without saying anything. Talon was right behind him. He waited for Talon at the hitching post where he had left his horses.

Talon was still smiling.

"You'll find any tack you need in the barn," said Ed. "Same room you'll be staying in. I'm going back to my fence."

Talon watched as Ed disappeared into the trees and then had a look around. He was feeling a little unsettled. He had hoped he might find some work along the way, but not so suddenly, and not like this. Still, the more he thought about it the more he liked it.

He thought of things he had seen among his own people and realized that as different as the two cultures were, these white people were, in many ways, not so different from his own. It made him feel a little more at ease with the situation and set him to work.

First, he found the tack room where Janice had said it would be and was happy to see that there was a small bed in one end of it. It even still had a mattress on it. The mice and chipmunks had been at it, and some of the stuffing was gone. Other than that, and a lot of dust, it was considerably better than the ground.

Talon brushed it off the best he could and dropped his bedroll onto it. The room had one window that looked across the corral and to the house beyond. It was caked in dust. Rain had packed it into mud on the outside. It took a few minutes, but he soon could see through it well enough to see anything he wanted to on the outside.

CHAPTER 4

THE SHIRT OFF HIS BACK

The first thing he had noticed was the horses. They were both mares, and neither had ever had their feet trimmed or shod. He had never needed to shoe a horse and wasn't ready to learn how. He would trim them as soon as he could, he told himself. First things first.

Looking around the room, he found a lariat. It was one of the things the white culture had brought that he had learned to like right away. It was stiff enough to retain the loop well when you threw it, yet strong enough to hold any horse he had ever worked. It was a little ragged out from years of wear but he could make it work.

The corral the mares were in was too large to work well in and had no anchor post to work from. That he knew would make things a little harder. He decided that the first order of business was to locate the strongest two posts in the corral and use them.

It was not the best because it meant he could get pinned between a panicked and fighting horse and the corral. That was something he would just have to work with, at least for the moment anyway.

The first mare he chose was the larger of the two and looked strong. She stood in the end of the corral with her nose in the corner, looking owl-eyed and ready to run. The corral was square. That was another problem he would have to work out. It gave the horses corners to nose into and that left the fighting end facing him. To solve the problem he stood far enough away to keep from being kicked and tossed a loop on the large bay. She didn't panic as much as she could have and just stood for a few seconds.

Then she tossed her head and ran for the other end of the corral. Talon kept the rope tight but didn't try to stop her. Soon enough she would realize who was in control.

When she got to the other end of the corral she stopped for just an instant and then broke again. This time when she got to the place she had started, she nosed her head into the corner behind the other mare. *Good,* thought Talon, *she is smart.* She was trying to use the other horse for a buffer between her and Talon. Talon waited a few seconds and then wrapped the lariat around his right side so as to sort of sit on it like one might lean into the seat of a swing. Then he leaned heavy on the rope with all his weight. At first, the mare refused to move but when the rope came tight on the back of the other horse it bucked and moved back. In an instant, the large bay was running again.

This time when she bolted past Talon he threw a loop into the lariat and tried to catch her foot. It missed but when she made her return he crowded her against the fence by moving into her way just enough to panic her into a full run. That put her front feet higher, and one of her feet became tangled in the loop. It was a trick that took a lot of practice and only worked after a few tries, even then.

When he realized he had her foot, Talon wrapped the rope under his hip again and leaned back hard. This took the mare's left front foot out from under her and caused her to fall. She regained herself with her back legs still upright, but her nose hit the ground. It made her snort in pain.

The loop came loose when she fell. As soon as she got her feet back she ran again. Over and over the game played on. The mare ran from one end of the corral to the other and Talon tried to trip her when he could. After a few times of being tripped the mare became more cautious about running past him. It meant he could no longer trip her. It also showed the mare that running was unless and could even be painful.

In an hour or so the mare found a corner and refused to move no matter how hard Talon pulled on the rope. *Gaining ground,* thought Talon. He leaned on the rope and held it for a few minutes.

The rope was choking the mare and she was uncomfortable but still refused to move. Talon moved closer. When he was close enough, the mare swapped her hind quarters around to square up with him. Any closer and she would be able to kick him. Talon smiled; he had been here before. She was running out of ideas and he was gaining control.

One of the stronger posts was a gate post. The mare chose the corner about ten feet from it. Talon lay down on the ground and rolled under the fence. From outside the fence, he wrapped the rope around the top of the post a couple times. Then he slid down the loose end of the rope until he was close enough to the mare to cause her to spook again. This time he was on the outside of the fence and she was getting more familiar with his presence.

She was a smart horse and was beginning to put things together. Talon spoke to her in as soothing a voice as he could.

The mare watched him approach with close study. When he was about four feet away she pulled back and tried to get back to the other end of the corral. When she did, Talon pulled the slack up in the rope until she got to the post.

As she approached the post, Talon sat down on his end of the rope again and pushed hard with his legs. The mare's head pulled hard to the top of the post.

She instantly realized her mistake and had a short panic. This time she was in an awkward position. Pulling from the top of the post was harder and she could not get her head down to gain leverage. She tried to sit down and use her weight and her hind legs to pull free, but that put her head higher and made it even harder to pull.

For a little while, she fought and kicked dust into the air with her hind legs. Then she stood and pulled hard on the rope until it was weakening her by cutting off her air. Talon watched and held his end of the rope and waited. After a minute or so of wheezing the look in her eyes changed to a pathetic, defeated look and she stepped forward one step and slacked the rope. She stood breathing hard for a spell and Talon let her keep the three feet or so of rope she had.

At that point he knew she had begun to realize what he already knew, he had the power to call the shots. He tied his end of the rope off, then left her standing and went for a long break.

The room he was about to use could use some cleaning and he needed to get unpacked. The mare needed time to think things over and the day was young. After he looked around a little he found another smaller corral where he left his own horses and set about the task of getting his pack and blankets into his new quarters.

As he was leaving the corral side, something moved above him on the barn wall. He only saw it with the corner of his eye, but that was enough. He stopped and studied the wall as best he could without looking straight at it.

When he did he realized that a knothole in the wall of the barn loft had suddenly lit up from the sun coming in through the roof vent. Someone had been watching him. It made him feel uneasy. He kept his eyes on the ground as he walked back towards the barn, not wanting whoever it was to know that he had seen them.

Once inside the barn, he looked at the soft earth on the floor near the north ladder that climbed into the loft. Finding nothing he walked the length of the barn to the south end. The barn was designed like many others. It was basically a long narrow passage with wide structures on either side and the loft over the entire structure for winter storage of hay. Both ends had double doors that were normally left open for ventilation. The south end was the end farthest from the corral. The only way to get to it was to go around the barn to the back. Or walk through it from the front.

It could be easily done from the back but one would need to climb a fence at the corner of the barn to do it. It wasn't a much-used way into the barn. That ladder had small boot tracks that came in from outside. They were the size of a woman's foot. Talon inspected the tracks and decided they were a bit smaller than what Janice would leave and not deep enough.

Janice, unless she would have changed them, wore ladies boots with a higher heel. These were more like riding boots. *Lacey,* thought Talon. Or someone he had not met yet. Not good. He thought of climbing the ladder to see who it was but decided that if it was Lacey, as he suspected, he might be better off to leave things as they were.

When he got back to his room he set about checking the ceiling for any peep-holes that might be used from the loft. The floor of the loft was the ceiling for the room where he slept. He found none, so he started knocking down dust and cobwebs. He found an old straw broom in the corner and swept the floor and was rolling out his bedroll when he heard Janice call from the front porch of the cabin.

"Talon," she called. Then before he could answer she called again. This time Talon stepped out from the barn where she could see him.

"Can you come in for a minute?" Said Janice. "I need measurements."

Talon nodded his head and shut the door to his room.

Lacey wanted to leave as soon as she saw Talon heading towards the barn from the corral but was afraid he might hear her walking on the board floor of the loft. She sat down instead with her back against the wall and waited.

She wanted to talk to Talon but didn't know where to begin. He was a couple years older than she was, but that wasn't a problem as far as she could see. The fact that he was an Indian wasn't a problem either. Not for her. It would be for everyone else she knew, well almost everyone else, and that was a problem.

Nevertheless, she liked how he looked and she especially liked watching him work. He was strong and interesting. He appeared as wild as the wind, maybe even a little dangerous, but she found him good looking. She was fairly certain that her dad would shoot him if he had the slightest notion that she was even thinking such things, but in Lacey's world, there were ways to do things that were not so much "in your face" as all that.

He hadn't said much at dinner but he hadn't been given much of a chance to.

She found the little war between her parents highly embarrassing, but nothing new. It was interesting that they would let it happen in front of a stranger though. She guessed that it was because Talon was an Indian. Like he didn't count for as much or something.

She decided she liked the way he had handled it. In fact, she found it a little humorous in a way. He just kept looking from one of her parents to the other, and his eyes just kept getting bigger. Then he started to eat like a passing freight train. She was sure he was blushing, but it was hard to tell.

It was right at the last when he smiled at her father that really won her over. He seemed happy.

She was still waiting when she heard her mother call for Talon to come in. It was a lucky break. The last thing she wanted was for Talon to know that she had been spying on him from the loft. It would be much too embarrassing. She watched as Talon entered the house and climbed back down the ladder.

She didn't like that she had been trapped in the loft and decided she would have to change her method next time.

Inside the house Talon found Janice standing by the sewing machine. She had a long cloth tape in her hands and stretched it out to suggest what she wanted. Talon smiled and walked over to where she was.

"Hold out your arm please," she said. "I need to see how long they are."

Talon held out his arm and waited. Janice looked into his eyes and smiled. It gave him an uneasy feeling. He had never been so close to a woman, other than his mother, especially one so close that he could smell her breath and the faint hint of her perfume.

"Nice," said Janice. "Twenty-four inches and I will need to leave room for those powerful arm muscles. They are the biggest I think I have ever measured."

They didn't seem all that big to Talon. No more than a lot of the men on the reservation. Janice pulled the tape around his upper arm and smiled again.

"Very nice," she said.

After that, she walked around to his back. He couldn't see her and was caught off guard by the feel of her hand on his shoulder. It made him flinch a little.

"Oh relax Talon," she said in a somewhat more than soothing voice.

"I won't bite you."

Talon wasn't sure about that, and hearing her say it did little for his comfort level. He felt her hand slide across his shoulder. It felt as though it was flat down, not holding the tape, but he couldn't tell.

"You know," she said. "I really can't tell much with all this leather on your back. I'm afraid you are going to have to take off your shirt. I hope you don't mind."

Talon did mind. He fought back a little panic and wondered if she could still make the shirt if he refused. Janice walked around to face him again and started to reach for the tail of his shirt.

"Really Talon," she said. "We who make clothes for men must do this all the time. Now just stand still. This won't take a moment."

Talon realized he was about to loose his shirt and there was little he could do about it. He raised his arms and Janice pulled up his shirt. She was nowhere tall enough to reach his hands and stepped close enough that her belly was tight against his.

She still could not reach his hands and Talon pulled them down in front of himself. Janice pulled the shirt off and laid it down on the table. She stood smiling at him for a second.

Then she put her hands on the upper part of his chest so that her thumbs touched when she spread her hands out. Talon's heart stopped. He had never been measured for a shirt before. His buckskins were hand-me-down's from his uncle. Even so, he wondered how much of all this was necessary. Still, he reasoned, I wouldn't want her to question how I break horses. He was sure his face was more red than ever and being embarrassed made him all the more embarrassed.

"Nice wide chest," said Janice.

It seemed her voice sounded softer than usual and maybe a little shaky.

"Now turn around," she said in somewhat stronger voice." I need to measure your shoulders again."

Talon did as she asked and soon felt her hands on his back. Once again her hand slid across his shoulders while she held the tape straight and took the measurement. Her skin was soft and would have been pleasant under other circumstances.

"Very good," she said.

She then gently brushed his ponytail out of her way and rested it on his shoulder as best she could.

She held the tape at the top of his spine and slid her hand slowly down until it touched his pant top. She held it there a moment and then let it fall free. Picking up a letter pad she recorded the measurements.

"In a couple of days," she said without looking up. "I will need to measure your inseam."

"Okay," said Talon.

Whatever that meant it sounded like he could put his shirt back on and that was good news.

"That's the inside of your leg, just to let you know. From your ankle to your... she paused, well just above your upper thigh."

Talon's eye's widened. *Just above my thigh? So where does my thigh end?* he thought to himself.

"I really must," said Janice. "I need it for your nice wool pants. You will find it all worth it, in the end, I'm sure."

Talon was beginning to wonder about that. He quickly put his shirt back on. It wasn't easy. Janice was standing so close that he found it hard to move freely.

"Yes ma'am," he said as he pulled it down around his waist. Janice smiled and stepped aside to let Talon by. "Thank you," Talon said as polite as he could.

The barn never looked so good. He had forgotten all about Lacey by the time he got back to his bunk. For the moment he had enough to keep his mind busy on other things. Things like the horses.

The mare he had tied was standing quiet. The sorrel was standing close by. Close enough to almost touch the larger mare. Talon had seen this before. It's almost like the free one is feeling compassion for the one who is tied. He had chosen the larger mare in the hope that she was the lead mare of the two. If he had found the other mare at the other end of the corral he would have known that he chose amiss. Seeing her there was good news.

After a quick search of the tack, he found a strong halter and tied about twenty feet of lead rope to it. He approached the corral as easy as he could and when he was a few feet away began to talk to the mare as soothing as possible. He wanted her to recognize his voice so was careful not to change it. He wanted her to feel safe around him, and to know him by sight or sound.

When he got close enough the smaller mare moved away. She didn't run but just walked to the other side of the corral. The mare Talon was working with was the lead mare between the two, the bell mare, and breaking her first would make the other one more approachable.

He wasn't concerned with the sorrel for the moment but was glad to see the way she reacted to the tying of the bay.

Talon made it all the way to the anchor post without the mare pulling back. She was watching him and looked a little spooked but she wasn't panicked.

Reaching over the rail he took the lariat in his hand and tried to pull the mare closer. She refused. Untying the rope on his end, he looped it around his hip and sat down on it again. The rope was still wrapped around the post and It was hard to gain any of it with the mare pulling on the other end. When he pulled she tried to fight free. In the scuffle, he was able to gain rope until her nose was touching the post.

The mare snorted but was not panicky. That let Talon start the next lesson. After he tied her off again he reached over the corral and fought the halter onto the mare's head and buckled it. The fight would have been all but impossible from the side of the corral the mare was on.

She threw herself first to one side of the post and hard up against the corral fence and then to the other, each time slamming up against the corral with enough force to hurt a man even if she didn't kick his brains out in the process.

Once the halter was securely in place Talon tied the lead rope to the top of the anchor post. He tied it close enough to keep her from getting good pulling leverage but not right up to the post. The slip-knot he used would let him free her when he wanted to, even if she was pulling back. Normally, getting this far would take more time and he was impressed at how fast she was getting it. He left and returned shortly with a burlap feed sack.

He climbed the corral a little way from the mare and walked up to her. She pulled away and pressed herself up against the corral. He was glad she didn't try to kick him, but it made him wonder. She wasn't fighting like a mustang usually does. He had worked horses that would try to bite him or kick him at any opportunity, even some who attacked him like a lion the instant he entered the corral. Those were some of the best horses once broken, but the hardest to break.

These horses had all the earmarks of mustangs but none of the fight, like barn horses that had been left to themselves since birth, but were familiar with humans.

When he was close enough he held the sack by one corner and began to flip it under her belly. The first time he did it she kicked at it and fought up against the corral fence. Moving closer he did it again, and she tried the other side. Talon moved out of the way and let her hit that side. Then he did it again. He kept doing it until she stopped fighting and stood still. He then threw it over her back and dragged it off. She quivered and jumped a little but didn't move. So he tried her belly again. She stood, so he talked to her as he walked up closer to her.

The mare was nervous and was quivering. She was up against the corral as tight as she could get but wasn't fighting. He reached out and touched her on the shoulder with the back of his hand. Soon he was able to pet her neck and part of her back.

Talon left for the tack room again and returned with a soft lead rope that felt like it might be made of cotton. On one end of the rope, he tied a loop like the one in the end of the lariat. He slipped the rope through the loop so that he had a noose that would close tight if pulled. Three feet or so up the rope he tied a loop in it that would not slip closed under pressure. What he had then was a rope with a sliding loop in one end and a small slip-less loop tied in the middle of it.

Talking softly, he slowly approached the mare until he was standing at her shoulder. He laid the untied end of the rope carefully over her neck until he could reach it on the underside. That end he slipped through the knot designed not to slip. It made a large loop that nearly touched the ground. The other end, the one with the noose, he pulled a wide enough loop into for her foot to fit through and let it rest on the ground.

When he was ready, he bumped the mare's fetlock with his foot. At first she did nothing, but when he kicked a little harder she picked up her foot and stepped forward. Now she was standing on the loop of the rope and that was not what he wanted so he tried again. This time he succeeded. She had stepped into the noose. Lifting up on the noose he pulled it tight around her leg just above her hoof and below her fetlock. The mare, when she felt the rope tighten, tried to stomp the loop off but when she lifted her leg to do it Talon was waiting. He snapped up hard on the rope by pulling it through the slip-less loop until the mare's foot was pulled up as far as it could go and anchored securely to her neck.

The mare tried to step down on the lifted leg but she couldn't. She tried to throw her weight on the raised leg and nearly fell over onto Talon. He held the rope and let her find her feet again. When she realized she was only on three legs she pulled hard on the tied leg and tried with rapid stomping motion to free her leg. Then she snorted a little and stood still.

Talon could see that she was more than a little unnerved and let her stand for a while. There was nothing else she could do. A horse on three legs is, for the most part, a helpless animal. Some of them will try to pull and now and then one might fall, but the situation is so foreign to them that they are not able to figure out what they should do about it. They only seem to know about life on all fours.

Talon had learned the trick from Falling Water

and used it to his advantage any time he was working with green horses. He was glad she had been born on the range; it made horses smarter to have to figure out how to survive in the wild. A smarter horse was a lot easier to work with.

The other mare had retreated to the far end of the corral and was standing watching from what she felt was as safe a distance as she could get.

Talon took the lariat off the lead mare and left the halter rope tied to the anchor post. There was no reason to worry that the mare would be able to pull with any success and even if she blew up all she would do was fall down. If she did, he would have to start all over again.

Watching the free mare, he worked a large loop in the rope and began to repeat the process he had used on the first horse.

The work day was about over by the time he had the smaller mare tied and got back to the other horse. She was standing still. The look on her face was that of a trapped animal. Talon walked up to her at a normal pace and began to run his hands all over her body. He rubbed her belly and brushed her mane and tail out with a curry comb he found in the barn. When he had all the burs combed from her mane and tail he continued to pet her all over.

She threw her head around and a couple times she tried to rare up. She tried to protect herself as best she could and threw herself up against the corral fence. Soon enough she gave up. He kept after her until she let him pet her forehead and brush out the long mane hair between her eyes. She didn't like it but she was not able to prevent it. Talon used that fact to force her to let him do as he wished.

All the time he worked her he talked to her. Before it was time for dinner she was standing, and her eyes were normal when he touched her. The hardest part was over.

A horse can learn a lot in a fairly short time if the work is done carefully. Trying to hurry too much can cause the animal to get frustrated and start rebelling. If that happens the war that results will cost more time and trouble than ever.

Knowing this, Talon let the bay have her leg back and untied the halter rope from the post. Then he dropped it on the ground and walked away. For a second the mare did nothing but in time she realized she was free and trotted to the other end of the corral, dragging the rope behind her.

Talon watched to see how she would handle the dragging rope. She wasn't sure what to do with it and Talon waited to see if she would do as some other horses had and try to outrun it. This one just turned around to look behind herself and stared at it.

It was time to work the other mare but before he could start, Ed came home. He was dusty and looked more tired than Talon felt. He rode up and tied his horse off to the stock tank hitching rail. Talon watched until Ed turned his way and then he went on with his work.

The sorrel was tied by then to the other gate post and wasn't liking it. She kept trying to rear up, but her head was tied down. Talon had been letting her cool when Ed rode by. He had her tied as close to the post as he could get her. It would be better he thought, to look busy so he worked a little closer to her. She threw herself against the corral and stood snorting.

Ed left his horse tied and stripped the saddle. Then he carried it to the corral and threw it over the rail.

"Looks like you got em started," he said.

"I do," said Talon. "You don't have another saddle I can use, do you? I can do without if need be, but it would be nice."

"I do," said Ed. "It's old but you can make it do. It's the one Lacey uses so you may need to adjust the stirrups. She hangs it in the other side of the barn by the silo. Who knows why?"

Ed seemed more than just tired. He seemed tired inside and out. Like he had begun to grow weary of the war that he had found himself in. Talon was glad he was only here for a short while.

The day was ending and the sun was low in the sky. Janice stepped out onto the porch to report that supper was ready and both men set out for the cabin.

Supper was a lot quieter than lunch had been. Talon watched as the food was handed around and took what he felt was right. He was able to eat more than he took but didn't want to seem greedy.

Ed was a thick man. Not fat, though at first glance you might confuse him for it. Given a closer look, he was just thick. He had massive arms and legs and a neck like a rutting buck.

Talon noticed that he was eating a lot quieter tonight. He wasn't saying much either and seemed lost in his thoughts. It left an almost uneasy feeling in Talon but he tried to ignore it. The rest of the cabin was about the same. He paid closer attention to the boots Janice wore. He had been right; they were not the boots that had left the tracks in the barn.

Everything in the cabin seemed perfectly placed and spotless. Janice seemed proud of that and handled everything as if it were made of the most precious material known to man. Talon thought it a little ridiculous but it was not something that he thought much on. She seemed to live in a world of her own and keep to herself, at least as long as she wasn't measuring him for clothes. Her mind seemed always busy behind her eyes in a world where she manufactured her own sort of devices, unseen devices that she used to build the platforms she hung her adversaries on. It allowed her to stay one step ahead. It was how she set up conversations to her advantage before they even happened. He hoped to never become one of her adversaries. It was how she manipulated Ed, who often knew it was happening but found it easier to play along than not.

He worried about that thing she warned him about with his pants. He was not looking forward to that. I can do it, he told himself. I will get new pants if I do it.

Lacey sat at her place next to Janice and ate in silence. She kept her eyes and no doubt her ears on constant alert for any sign of another table-side battle between her parents. First, she would look at her father and then at her mother. Then she went back to eating. It reminded Talon of how dogs act when they are waiting for a storm.

Once she noticed Talon was looking around the table and smiled. Then she tossed her hair back and smiled again. Talon tried not to let her know he noticed. In truth, there wasn't much he didn't notice.

"I have your shirt well started," said Janice. "I would like you to let me hold it up next to you for a look at the fit after supper."

She was smiling at Talon. It made him feel like she was expecting something from him but he wasn't sure what. He decided to just smile back and hope that was enough.

"You will stay after won't you?" she asked, after a moment."

"Yes ma'am," said Talon a little shaky.

He looked around but it didn't seem anyone else was even listening. Eating at the white man's table would take a little practice, he decided. Especially if Ed was the only teacher he could look to for help.

Supper went smooth and after he ate, Ed sat down in the chair by the stove and stretched out his legs without saying anything. He was only a few feet from the brightly colored bolts of cloth. Janice and Lacey cleared the table and put the dishes in the sink.

Janice then went to the sewing table and motioned for Talon to join her there. Talon walked over to where she was and stood waiting.

"Here we are," she said.

She held up what looked like the back of a shirt and had other parts laid out on the table. It looked like she had already sewn the sleeves closed. As she held up the shirt back Talon stared in wonder at the cloth. It was a beautiful red plaid pattern and had black lines that separated the squares. The material had a new look that would make it even more beautiful when it was finished. He touched the tail of the shirt back. He couldn't resist it. The feel was as rich as the look. She had chosen a high-quality wool. It was heavy but not too heavy, and in his working hands it felt soft.

"Do you like it?" she asked.

"Very much," said Talon. "I never realized."

He stopped without saying more. He was afraid

of making a fool of himself. Words couldn't tell how it felt anyway. He was amazed at the thought that it would be his.

"That will be all for now," said Janice, as she stepped back from behind Talon. She was smiling when he turned around to thank her and leave. Her eyes seemed to say more than her smile suggested but he excused it for nothing more than his own thoughts.

It felt good to be outside again and free from Janice and the cabin. He wasn't that fond of closed places that had no good way out from any side, like a lodge had. Cabins were a white man thing. They were a lot warmer in the winter and nicer to live in than sleeping on the ground, but they were foreign to him and he was always glad to get back outside.

The horses were right where they had been when he left. He wished he had more time with the sorrel but knew that there would be time later. He had her tied and when he found a suitable halter for her he fought it onto her head. Then he let both horses wander around dragging the lead ropes he had tied to them.

Chapter 5

Cotton Bait

Daylight was creeping into the meadow when Talon came awake. The sun would not be up for a while but the Barred Rock rooster in the nearby coop was already at it. The brighter it got, the more he crowed.

Talon watched the mares through the little window in his room. It was full summer now and the days were warm. The grass in the meadow moved lightly in a breeze that seemed to come from nowhere and fade into the trees. There were a few mule deer on the far end of the meadow, three fat little does and a new fawn. They began lifting their heads and looking around as the day approached. A little while later they retreated back into the cover of the surrounding forest. He watched as the last one wandered silently away and out of sight. An owl drifted across the meadow and landed in the top of the barn where it spent its daylight hours. The world was coming awake.

Someone moved inside the cabin but he couldn't see who it was. A moment later smoke began drifting up from the chimney.

After he rolled his bedroll, he left it on his bed and walked out to where the mares were standing. He forked a good pile of hay into the corral and then went and fed his own horses. When he returned, the mares were feeding and didn't seem concerned in the least that he was near. Slipping through the rails of the corral he moved quietly up behind the larger mare and picked up her lead rope. He expected her to pull away and try to run. All she did was throw her head to try to gain a little slack in the rope. So

Talon moved a little closer, keeping the rope tightly in his hands in case she did decide to bolt.

He began talking to her and moving slowly closer. When he was close enough, she moved a little sideways and raised her head to watch him. She wasn't afraid, but she didn't quite trust him either.

After a moment she went back to eating. It impressed him how quickly she had become accustomed to him and he decided to see how far he could push her. Most horses would still be pretty crazy after only one day of work but this one was putting things together quick. He wondered if it was the trick with the tied front leg that broke her. Like she had decided that he was her superior and was able to take her ability to fight or escape from her.

She was smarter than he had seen a horse in a long time, but even a smart horse should be spookier than she was. He wondered if someone had been petting her, or maybe feeding her treats or something. Then he thought of Lacey. The horses had been on the place for a while. *That would make sense*, thought Talon.

He moved a little closer and now was only about four feet from her head. She pulled back on the rope, but not hard, and Talon held it tight, expecting a fight. He had been watching her ears to try to anticipate her next move when he suddenly realized that she was shifting her eyes from him to something behind him and a little to his left.

"Mornin Lacey," said Talon.

Keeping his hold on the rope he turned to look at her. He wasn't that surprised that it was her. Lacey had slipped up behind him and was standing on the bottom rail of the corral watching him work. Her hair was down. It was waist length, and thick enough to be pleasant to look at. It was a little too showy for Talon and made him wonder what her mother might think if she knew. Lacey wasn't that much younger than Talon, maybe sixteen or so, but seemed like someone from another world to him. He found her hard to read. She was quiet and looked down a lot. Without being able to see her eyes or face well, he was left a little in the dark.

She seemed abnormally quiet around her mother and said as little as possible, but that all seemed to change when she looked at Ed. If she saw him looking at her, she suddenly put on a playful look. Talon got the impression that it was by design — her method of survival maybe, or maybe just simple manipulation. Either way, he figured it got her what she needed. At least so long as Janice wasn't in the way.

Janice it seemed was more a loose canon, as they say, than even Ed. Lacey could make Ed as moldable as clay, but it was the only time Talon saw him with a real smile on his face. She was definitely her daddy's little girl. How they looked at each other wasn't a problem for Talon. What bothered Talon was how she looked at him, like a young woman. Not shy enough for his taste.

This time he could see her eyes. They were the color of the sky on a clear summer day and filled with mischief. She tossed her head, and her hair lifted and fell across her back.

"That's amazing," she said.

Talon turned back to the mare. He wished she wasn't there. He liked working alone.

"Is it time to eat?" He asked

"Almost. What did you do to make her so gentle?"

"Nothing. She just is, or someone has be-friended her."

"Well she wasn't before, but she was getting bet-ter. She let me pet her on the nose sometimes."

Talon was a little nervous about being alone with the daughter of Janice Clanton, even if they were out in the open. He didn't want to take the time to try to explain his process anyway. Besides that, he wasn't sure Lacey hadn't already started the horses a little before he got there.

The bay had acted as if she had become accus-tomed to humans and didn't have much fear to overcome from the start. The sorrel should be flightier than she was also. The horses were not totally green. So far the bay was the only one he had worked with. She didn't like being made to do things, but she realized a little too easy who was in charge.

It would make his job a lot simpler. What to do about Lacey was another problem. The last thing he wanted to do was make waves with Janice. On the other hand, he realized that the way into or out of the family circle was standing on the bottom rail of the corral staring at him with bright blue eyes.

Talon really didn't want either one — the family, or the dressy looking blond. He just wanted his clothes and an open trail. Anyway, if he had wanted a woman in his life it wouldn't be this one. She was white, and that could get him shot. Besides that, white folk seemed too soft to him. *Still,* he told himself, *she is a fine girl to look at.* He put that thought away as fast as it had arrived.

A man's voice called out from the porch. It was Ed.

"Breakfast," he said.

Talon could see from the look on Ed's face it wasn't all he meant to say. Lacey pulled that smile out as fast as a gunslinger and fired it straight at Ed.

"Okay," she said, and half ran to the house like she had been caught at something she knew he might not approve of. Talon let the lead rope drop and started in the direction of the house. Ed stopped him on the porch.

"Don't know you very well," said Ed, "and don't really want to start any trouble with ya, but just in case you couldn't figure it out for yourself, I ain't interested in having no Injun for a son in law. Don't mean I don't like ya. Just sayin."

Talon smiled and nodded his head. "Yes sir, Mr. Clanton," he said and went on into the house.

Lacey was nowhere to be seen once Talon got inside. She came out of one of the back rooms shortly after. He noticed her hair was in a bun. She smiled at him but said nothing.

Janice was at the stove. She had cut the biscuits from the night before in half and was toasting them face down on the top of the stove. As usual, the cabin smelled good. It was a homey sort of smell he liked but could not feel truly welcome in. A little like looking in through a glass window at smiling faces you couldn't ever touch. He didn't mind. It was as it should be. He was a guest, nothing more, just like he liked it.

Ed was right behind him. He hung his hat on a buck rack nailed to the wall and sat down at the table. Talon was already seated. Janice was the last one to the table. She had fried eggs and bacon on a large platter in the center of the table. She brought the fried biscuits with her and sat down to eat.

"Your shirt will be nearly finished by suppertime." She told Talon.

"That's very nice," said Talon. "You're a fast worker."

He had no way of knowing how long it might take to make a shirt, but he was surprised at how soon she was expecting to have it finished.

He was excited about the shirt, but he remembered that inseam thing every time he thought about it. He looked over at the machine on the distant wall.

His shirt had been laid out on the table at one end of it. It really was a beautiful shirt and he could hardly believe his good fortune. In fact, it was a little too good to be true. He put that out of his mind along with all the rest and ate his food.

The day turned out to be clear and warm. Turtle doves cooed and swooped from the top of the barn to the nearby trees. Had they known there was an owl inside they would not have been around. Or maybe they did know. Animals seem to sense when to run. Little songbirds hopped along the edge of the water trough and dipped their small beaks into the cool fresh water for a drink. All in all, it looked like a good day to be on the trail. *But not today,* thought Talon as he made his way to the corral.

The larger mare was coming along so well that he decided to try Lacey's saddle on her. He found it where Ed had told him to look, and there was a head rig with it. That was something he had forgotten. He needed to fight the bit into the first horse's mouth. He hoped she was smart enough to learn to take it without too much trouble.

In the end, he had been right. The big mare stood at the end of the corral, shaking her head up and down trying to spit the bit out, as Talon set his sights on the sorrel. She had walked over to where the bay was and stood about ten feet down the corral fence.

Talon picked up the lariat and flipped a large loop into the business end of it. He was standing between the two mares. The sorrel threw her head and trotted to the other end of the corral. The motion of Talon's arm had spooked her a little and she wanted a little distance between them. Neither horse was as spooky as wild horses would have been. Talon attributed that to the fact that they had been on the property for long enough to become accustomed to people. Lacey feeding and petting them had also made a big difference. It had started them thinking that humans were a good thing and not to be feared.

The sorrel had learned to get along well with the lead rope dragging behind her, and he could have used it to catch her with, but he wanted to see her reaction to his arms swinging in the air to throw the rope. He wanted her to be unafraid enough not to panic at the motion. He watched her as he got closer to where she was standing.

At first she did nothing, but when he was close enough she suddenly laid her ears back and bolted. As she squeezed by between Talon and the fence he tossed the loop of the lariat over her head and leaned back hard on the rope. As soon as it came tight she stopped and turned toward him.

So, thought Talon, *who are you?* He began working his way up the rope. As he did he realized how pleased with life he was feeling. This was what he lived for — the smell of the horses, the warm sun, and getting to know new friends like these two.

The bay was starting to show signs of liking him. She was smart, the leader type. She was a horse that would leave the barns behind and not feel separation anxiety over it. The sorrel was a good horse as well, he decided, but not a leader. She would make a good packhorse but could be used for anything someone had the time and patience to teach her. He liked them both.

The sorrel stood motionless as he approached her until he was about four feet away and then she bolted again, but not as fast. Talon held the rope but didn't try to stop her. The fourth time they played those same steps the mare stopped running. She was getting tired and started looking for another way to deal with the situation.

She had chosen the bay and had put herself between the larger mare and the fence at the end of the corral. Talon let her stand for a little while and cool down. Then he pulled the rope tight. As he did, it lifted up against the rump of the bay.

He expected the big mare to spook and at least lunge forward, but all she did was turn sideways up against the corral fence and leave the sorrel without a hiding place. At that, the sorrel put her nose into the corner and showed Talon her fighting end.

Well enough, thought Talon. He worried that the two horses might become tangled if a fight broke out between him and the sorrel, but used the same methods he had used on the bay in spite of it.

An hour or so later, he had the sorrel tied to a post at the other end of the corral gate. He sacked her down and then let her stand on three legs while he tried a new thing with the bay.

He thought it must be about noon when he went to the barn to get Lacey's saddle. He thought about tying one leg up to put it on her but decided to wait and see what she would do first. He put the saddle on the top rail of the corral and approached the mare slow and easy.

When he got to her he began by letting her smell the saddle blanket he was about to use. She snorted a little but didn't pay much attention. A short time later, he began brushing her back and rump with the flat of his hand. After that he let the blanket down onto her back and positioned it gently into place.

It was at this point that he expected her to try to shake it off if she was going to, but she didn't seem to mind. He did the same with the saddle. When he pulled the cinch up she looked a little concerned and her ears laid back. *Here we go,* thought Talon. He tightened the cinch and started to fold the cinch knot into place when she lost some of her nerve and moved away from him.

"Easy," said Talon.

The big mare tried to look around to see what was on her back but was stopped by the lead rope. She was a little owl-eyed, and Talon waited for her to get used to the weight of the saddle on her back. She looked at him and began to realize that whatever he had placed on her back was not part of him. She wasn't sure she liked it. It was something new to learn to trust.

She shook her body, but the cinch was too tight to let the saddle fall. A moment passed and she stood looking forward like she was trying to make some sense of things. Then she snorted, began pulling back hard on the fence and tried to rear up, but both motions were stopped by the lead rope. Talon kept talking to her, and after a little while the sound of his voice caught her attention, and she stood and watched him for a few seconds.

That was a good thing. He walked slowly to her side, talking to her and began petting her neck. After a little while, he grabbed the saddle horn and pulled gently on it to let her know it was him and he meant no harm.

He was busy, and Ed riding up caught him by surprise. He had come for the noonday meal. Ed's feet had hardly hit the ground when Janice called out through the open door. It was time to eat.

Both horses were standing and looking good when Talon got back to the corral after eating. He wanted to ride the bay. He was sure he could. She was doing well. He worked the sorrel a little more and brushed out her mane and tail. Then he ran his hands over her like he had the bay. After that, he returned to the bay and rubbed her down as well. She was standing on all fours and he was careful about how he worked. Then back to the smaller mare and so forth. The time passed without his notice.

He was just thinking of stepping into the saddle on the bay when he caught a movement to his left. The wind had lifted something that wasn't there before. He looked over and saw Lacey standing at the end of the porch. The wind had lifted her hair and she brushed it from her eyes. It looked as though she had come out to watch. He didn't think it was time for dinner yet. Ed had not come home and the sun was still a little too high.

Talon nodded his head in her direction and turned his attention back to the mares.

"Mama needs you," she said as he turned back to his work.

Needs me, thought Talon. He doubted she might need help with anything. The moment had no doubt come. It was that inseam thing. He could feel it in his bones. He nodded his head again.

"Okay," He said." Be right in."

Strange what a man is challenged by, thought Talon. He would rather step into the saddle of a totally green horse than have Janice sliding her hand up the

119

inside of his leg. But worse things have happened, he decided and started for the cabin.

Lacey followed him into the cabin. He couldn't decide if that was good or bad. Janice was standing by her sewing machine with her little flexible tape in her hand. Talon was between her and Lacey. It reminded him of the bay mare when he put the saddle on her, only this time he was the horse.

Janice was smiling. "Talon," she said cheerfully, "your shirt is finished."

Good, thought Talon. *It's the shirt.* He had almost forgotten about the shirt. He suddenly smiled himself. He had thought of it a hundred times since he first saw it. Now as she held it up he liked it even more than before. It was not something he took lightly.

A fine new shirt was only a dream and he still couldn't understand entirely how it had come to be. It was hard to believe that someone would give him such nice things for so little effort on his part. He hoped it was simply because they could, and maybe

Ed really didn't know what to do with the mares.

"Well, don't just stand there. Come try it on," Janice said. Her voice sounded as if she was as excited as he was.

Talon suddenly felt oddly welcome to be in the house alone with the two women. It felt a little like one might feel if he had been suddenly adopted.

What a strange feeling, thought Talon. It was a comfortable feeling. Both women were smiling and looking very happy. Talon walked over to where Janice was standing, with Lacey close behind. He wasn't too sure what to do next and just stood looking a little sheepish. Janice could see he was a little uncertain.

"Here," she said.

She laid the shirt on top of the sewing machine and turned back to Talon.

"The first thing we need to do is get rid of this."

She reached over and grabbed the tail of Talon's buckskin shirt. Then with one smooth motion, she lifted it up. Talon raised his arms and let her pull the shirt as far up as she could reach. He had spent his entire life bare-chested in the village he was raised in, but somehow this felt very different. It made him a little embarrassed.

"Nice," said Lacey, her voice a little lower than usual.

Janice shot a warning glance at her.

"The shirt, I mean," she said quickly.

Then she smiled at Talon. He was getting that flight or fight panic again. Mostly flight.

"Here," said Janice.

She had the shirt and began putting Talon's arm into it like one might dress a child. Talon returned his attention to the beautiful shirt. He truly was excited. He turned around to let her continue helping him into it. Then she reached to the bottom of the shirt and began to button it up.

He realized for the first time that the buttons were made of shiny brass. He reached for one to inspect it more closely. It had an anchor on it like the one on a ship. He wasn't sure that's what it was but he didn't care. It was as shiny as a new coin and went perfectly with the material of the shirt.

"I hoped you would like them," she said. "It was what I had."

"I like them very much," said Talon.

He ran his hand down the front of the shirt as Janice adjusted the collar.

"There," she said, stepping back. "It looks very nice on you."

Talon could feel that he was all but beaming with joy. It made him feel rich. He wished he could wear it through the village just one time. He wanted to show what a fine thing it was to the people he had left behind.

That, he knew would not be possible. His thoughts were suddenly interrupted by the sound of Janice's voice.

"Now," she said. "I need to start the pants and the first thing I will need is that inseam measurement I mentioned the other day. Talon stiffened a little. Lacey moved around to where she was looking at Talon face on to watch. Janice knelt and held the tape to the bottom of Talon's pant leg. Then just as he expected she began sliding her hand with the tape in it up the inside of his leg. Talon swallowed and waited.

A second later she had reached the critical point. Her hand was literally at the crotch of his pants but she was off to one side enough that she wasn't measuring the actual inside of his crotch but was holding the tape on his leg a few inches away.

Talon's face must have made his fears obvious. He glanced at Lacey as Janice finished her work.

Lacey's face looked like one big smile and her blue eyes sparkled. Without making a sound, she mouthed the word. "Nice."

Talon looked quickly away. Janice had not stood up just yet but appeared to be finished. Talon stepped back as she rose.

"There," she said." Now that wasn't so bad was it?" Talon let his breath out and began breathing again.

"And now all I need is your waist size," said Janice.

She held the tape at the front of Talon's pants.

"Lacey," she said. "I need you a moment."

Lacey moved closer.

"Here," she said. "You hold the tape in the front for me."

Lacey smiled up at Talon and took the tape. At first, she tried to just hold it in place in the front of his pants, but then to secure it better she slipped two fingers into the top of Talons pants and trapped the tape between her fingers and thumb. Talon was a little taken back but realized why she might need to do things that way. It was how much she seemed to enjoy it that bothered him.

Janice wrapped the tape around him and pulled it snug.

"There," she said finally. The pants should go a little quicker than the shirt did. A little bit less complicated." She turned to record the measurement onto a piece of pattern paper near the machine.

"You know," she said. "A strong young man like you will no doubt wear out a nice outfit like this in a short time. It's too bad you won't be close by when it finally does happen. I could make you more that way."

"Yes ma'am," said Talon.

He wasn't entirely sure what she meant, but he was sure there was more to it than her words were exposing.

Talon was glad to be back at the corral, as he stood next to the bay mare. He couldn't decide what had just happened and dared not think what it sounded like Janice was saying. He decided she must mean that it would be good if he were to settle someplace close. That way he could work off more clothes when he needed them.

Not for me, thought Talon. *I have a new home and a new life and this place isn't it.*

He spoke softly to the bay mare and then put one foot into the stirrup. She did nothing, so he hefted his weight into it a little. The mare laid her ears back a little but stood still. Very carefully Talon swung his leg over the saddle and slowly sat down in the seat. The mare snorted and stepped around a little, but offered no fight. For a good bit he let her stand with his weight on her back and did nothing, then he rocked back and forth for a little.

When he felt she was good with it, he stepped down and then up again. For the next twenty minutes or so he got on and then off the mare. She didn't seem to like it much, but She wasn't alarmed at the process, so the moment of truth had arrived. Talon reached the lead rope, loosed it, and tucked a loop of it into the top of his pants in case he might find himself on the ground and need it.

The rest of the day was spent slowly riding around inside the corral on the mare. At first, Talon used a plow rein method of turning her but in the course of time, he began to teach her how to neck rein. Other than being nervous and a little jumpy, the big bay mare took it all in stride.

"Tomorrow is for you," Talon said as he untied

the sorrel. He led her around the corral for a while and let her pull back when she felt threatened, but held the rope while she did. The idea was to keep her from succeeding at pulling back. By staying with her, no matter where she went, he hoped she would realize pulling was not an effective weapon. If she pulled free and ran, Talon waited till she stopped and caught the rope again and started over. If he had pulled back too hard on the rope and then let her win the tug-of-war, it might be a step in the wrong direction.

CHAPTER 6

A COTTON CAGE WITH GOLDEN BARS

The sun was just below the horizon when daylight woke Talon from sleep. The room was still not well lit from the little window, but he could see to get dressed. He had not slept well. The night had been full of dreams. Now he lay and tried to remember them.

All he could recall was that they were of the clothes and mostly of Lacey. She was a very real problem. He had to find a way around the feelings that were beginning to eat at him. The truth was that she was beautiful. It was her hair that kept him from sleep he realized. Admit it or not, it was something to see. It made him want to run his hands through it, like spun gold. He realized that she used it to her advantage even in his dreams.

She was becoming a little like alcohol. A very small amount would be all she needed to intoxicate him.

He had seen what women could do to a man, while he was growing up in the village. People had lost everything over them, even their lives. The more alcohol came in, the worse it got. Not just the women either, everyone.

This one was especially bad. Had she forgotten herself? He was an Indian. No one would know, or care if he wound up swinging from a tree. Besides that, he was not ready to settle down. He had nothing to offer a woman and didn't want the responsibility. Anyway, he hadn't left home to stop half way to where he had set out for. It would ruin everything. Even had she been Indian he would not want her.

He was beginning to feel like a small bird who had been baited into a cage. In his mind's eye, he could see the shadows of the little bars in the door closing behind him. The feeling threatened him. That's what his dreams had been, he realized - the door of the cage slowly closing behind him. Fly, he told himself. I need to fly. She was a huntress, and one not to be ignored. Lacey was a young woman who had become used to getting what she wanted.

Talon rose and looked out the little window. Hard to his right, stood his own horses. The proud cut was looking at him. He seemed to be calling. *Just go*, thought Talon. *Gather up your things and go. What would be the worst that could happen?*

Then he thought of the beautiful shirt and fine warm pants. *I can do this*, he reasoned. *Just be on guard. I'm a man. Just ignore her, and Janice too. Keep my eyes on a cabin made of stone and a rich land.* The sorrel was doing well. Talon had become accustomed to the horses. They were easier than some he had worked but rare as it was, he had seen others like them. Half the battle was gaining their trust. Lacey had softened them for that.

He had rubbed the sorrel down while she stood on all four feet earlier in the day and she had let him lift one of her front feet. Now she stood tied and waited as Talon rode the bay.

It was an easy day so far. Breakfast had been mostly uneventful, except for a comment or two about the clothes. The pants would be finished by day's end, and so would the bay. She would be green and need to be ridden more but usable.

The sorrel would not be far behind her. Noon came and went and Talon left off the bay and started work in earnest on the sorrel. He put the bit in her mouth and fought the head rig onto her head. She had fought hard against it, and it was work, but in the end, he had managed it. She was trying to spit it out and was throwing her head around when Talon began working the saddle onto her back. He was feeling pressured and needed to be finished.

She accepted the saddle without much trouble, but Talon didn't trust her to step into it yet. He liked it best if a horse never learned to buck. He had seen horses who grew old and died, without ever bucking the first time. If they never started, it seemed, they just never got the idea.

It was not long before supper when he saw Lacey coming his way. She was coming from the barn. He thought that strange and then realized that the corral he was in was not easy to see from inside the cabin. You needed to walk out onto the porch to see it. The route she had chosen would keep her from being noticed by her mother. *Not a good sign*, thought Talon.

"You've been busy," she said as she approached the corral. He had turned his back to her and was tugging gently on the saddle horn and rocking the saddle back and forth. The mare looked like she might be about to blow up and he worried that he could be pushing her a little too fast. He backed away a few steps and spoke softly to her for a moment. When it seemed she was a little better, he turned his attention to Lacey. He didn't like that she had come, but he was resolved as to how to handle things and was ready, he thought, for the visit.

"Yes," he said, without turning around. "They are easy horses, quick to learn. I think they will be good-natured animals in time. They will need to be ridden though, every day if possible."

He turned to face Lacey. "How is your day going?"

"Not bad," said Lacey, "Been busy til now. You were riding the bay today. Impressive I'd say."

"She is a good horse. I like her."

"She has a good horseman to thank for that, I would say. It makes me wonder what else you might be good at."

Talon looked over at her. He didn't quite know what to say. Her hair was down again, and it framed her face well. She seemed to be trying to look a little forward. Her blue eyes were wide and bright. She was wearing a mischievous little smile she hoped would bring him closer. Talon smiled a little himself. It was a tease, but he caught himself enjoying it a little.

"Riding," he said, "I'm good at riding."

And that, he told himself, is what I plan to be doing as soon as I can.

"Well that's a great idea," said Lacey. "I like riding myself. We could go riding together. You could use the bay and I could borrow one of your horses."

He hadn't seen that coming. *Walked right into it,* he thought to himself. She is her daddy's daughter. I should pay more attention to where I'm going around here.

"I don't think the bay is ready to leave the corral yet, he said. "Besides, my horses are a little strong-willed and not easy to handle for a lighter person."

He was lying on both accounts but she had him at a bit of a disadvantage.

"Really," said Lacey. He could tell she was on to him.

"I think we could manage them," She said. "Especially you. You're a horseman extraordinaire."

"Maybe later," said Talon.

"Well okay," she said, "later then."

"You don't wear your hair down much in the cabin," said Talon. "A little too warm in there is it?"

"I think you know better than that," she said. "My mother is a little, shall we say, "strong willed" about some things. Like how I wear my hair, and who I talk to."

"You mean," said Talon, "she wouldn't like you wearing your hair down, or talking to me either."

"Oh no," said Lacey, "she likes me talking to you. She just wouldn't like me to let Daddy see me doing it – either one actually. Especially talking to you alone with my hair down."

He really hadn't been ready for that. For a moment he was dumbfounded. His mind instantly drifted back to the conversation during the shirt fitting. He had been right to be concerned. Janice had meant to say she wanted him to stay. He now realized that she might have wanted it for more than one reason. Good help is hard to find Falling Water was fond of saying. *And good son-in-laws,* thought Talon, *must be even harder.*

"She don't mind you talking to me?" He asked.

"Not at all," said Lacey. "She thinks you would make a fine son-in-law. Said she had been trying to think of a way to marry me off for years. Then there you were, big as life, standing at the stock tank. Just like God had dropped you from the sky.

"Daddy, on the other hand, isn't quite so easy to charm, but I can make Daddy dance from across the room if you haven't noticed. I think Mama feels a little caged up with me around and would like things the way they were before I arrived. "From the way they treat each other, I sometimes wonder if I wasn't the reason they got together in the first place. Sort of begs the question which came first, the chicken or the egg."

He decided to let that one slide by. He had already seen enough of Janice to wonder about a few things himself.

"Do you realize," asked Talon, "that your way of

talking to men leaves you looking a little like a bar-maid?" He paused. "Not to disrespect you. It just does."

"Do tell," said Lacey. "So, how many barmaids have you talked to?"

She had him there. He smiled a little.

"Well, not many," He admitted. "Just how I think they might talk." She laughed a little. Her eyes were lit up, and she looked like she was about to laugh out loud.

"I'm not offended," said Lacey. "I guess I meant for it to. I don't have much time. I'm afraid I've grown tired of the battle zone. If I don't strike while the iron is hot, I might not at all. You will be gone in another day or so. Then what shall I do?"

Talon could see her problem. Fortunately, that was indeed her problem, not his. He liked Lacey, but not well enough to die for her.

"I think you are overlooking something," he said." I'm an Indian, and your daddy already mentioned that to me."

"Well that's Daddy's problem," she said." I can

handle him. You needn't worry about that."

"Not just him," said Talon." A man like me would be dead inside a hundred miles with you."

"I don't think so," she said." I think you could cut your hair, change your clothes and pass yourself off as a white man quite easily."

She smiled again, then added, "If not, I figure I could just tell everybody that you're the captain of a fleet of ships who came all the way from Barcelona, Spain to whisk me away."

They both laughed at that. Talon had no idea where Barcelona Spain was but he got the point. His complexion was more like a dark-complected white than any shade of red. From the Lakota perspective, he was considered light-complected.

"My hair," said Talon, "is a sign of manhood in my world. It won't be cut off. I like nice clothes like the ones Janice makes, but they are for looking good in. I live in leather."

He didn't want to hurt Lacey, but she was not hearing him.

"You wouldn't cut it even for me?" she asked.

"No offense," said Talon, "but I'm not sure I would want to be with you. I don't even know you."

He expected her to be insulted by that, but he needed a hole in the cage. She was standing in the door, so to speak. Talon had turned to the mare again and was waiting for her to respond. She didn't. He turned, thinking he might have slipped through the bars, but she was gone without a sound.

An instant later he saw why. Ed had just broke from the trees and was coming in for supper.

So, thought Talon. *Now I know. Janice and Lacey are both looking for a hole in the same cage. They don't want me in the family so much as they want me to open doors for them to fly through.* Ed was another thing. Talon was pretty sure that Ed would cheerfully shoot him over Lacey. Lacey was mistaken about that, he figured. There is a place in a man where he will draw a line and a gun, and Lacey was Ed's.

What a mess, thought Talon. He doubted that Ed had any idea what the women in his life were up to, or how they felt about him. In a way, it made him feel sorry for Ed, but in the end, it was Talon himself he was becoming concerned for.

Both women seemed to be of the same mindset. This wasn't going to be easy, he told himself. Turns out he was right. Things were a little too good to be true. He wondered how much Janice knew of whatever progress Lacey might be making with him.

He noticed Lacey had come to the corral from the barn. She wanted to hide her tracks from Janice, but why he didn't know. He wondered if Janice really did want to be rid of Lacey or if Lacey just wanted things to look that way for his benefit. Another possibility was that Lacey was just happier keeping her movements private for purposes of her own. Privacy allows flexibility. Janice would know as much as Lacey wanted her to.

It made him wonder how much Ed knew. Maybe he was smarter than they thought. Smart enough to know to keep his head down. *Must be tough,* thought Talon, *living with a woman you don't really like and who doesn't seem to like you much either.* All the more reason to leave the Clanton place just like he found it, Alone. The trail never looked so good.

Ed rode in, looking hunted as usual. He had every bird and tree spotted on his way, and must not have been looking at the barn or cabin at all. Talon wondered if Ed was a little too nervous about his neighbor. He hadn't seen any sign of trouble with anyone since he arrived.

Ed might do well, thought Talon, *to spend more time keeping up with things at home.* But that was Ed's problem and he didn't want it to become his.

How to avoid that was becoming harder by the minute. It was easy to see that Lacey had plans of her own, and he was convinced she was up to something. It was possible, he reasoned, that she was doing what she could with the mares for some kind of escape plan of her own. If that was the case, he realized that he had just played into her hands in a way he could not have seen coming. That worried him all the more, and it made sense too.

He didn't like trying to understand these women. Any other white women would be avoiding him like a dead animal. That's what he was used to. Either these were desperate women, or they were just playing games. All he knew was that they had looped him in, and he was beginning to feel the rope.

Talon followed Ed to the cabin. He had not said anything since he arrived and Talon had only nodded his head when Ed rode up. He looked tired as usual and dusty. No one had called them in yet, but Ed was going in anyway so Talon followed. Janice had been in the back room when they came in and came out when she heard the door shut.

"Talon," she said cheerfully, "I'm glad you're here. Your clothes are ready."

That was the best news Talon had heard in a while. Janice motioned him over to the sewing machine. She had left the pants folded on the table that the machine was built into and picked them up. The fabric was stone gray in color and made of wool. Talon smiled. They were perfect in every way.

143

He had never seen pants this nice before, and the only time he had ever seen any pants like these they were worn by white men with money. Other people used wool pants but they were a more sack-like looking quality.

The loose fit was good in some ways. They allowed more unrestricted movement, but they were not made to fit. They were designed to allow one size to fit a lot of people and were not nearly as well made as these pants were. These were tailored to fit Talon and no one else.

"You need to go try them on," said Janice."

She handed the pants to him. Talon looked at his hands before he touched them. The last thing he wanted was to get them dirty. They were more than he could have ever expected to own. If he had the money he would not have spent it on tailored pants and shirt. What he would do with such fine clothes he didn't know. He had seen men robbed for clothes like these. To him, they were more valuable than money. Talon took the clothes back to his room to try them on.

The day was losing light, but he could easily see the horse tail hair he had tied to the door and to a split of wood on the outside wall of the room. It was tied with a slip knot for easy removal. He wasn't expecting anyone to go in when he wasn't there, but he liked the privacy of knowing no one had. The room was getting dark and he hurried into the new clothes. He liked the shirt tucked in. The pants fit perfectly enough for him to wear them without a belt. Janice had done a fine job. When he had dressed he left the room again and retied the horse hair as before.

Janice was waiting when he got back to the cabin.

"Very nice," she said. "Turn around now, so I can check out the other side."

She wanted to be sure that the cuff of the pants didn't lift in the back. They needed to be long enough, but not too long. They were perfect.

"Just as I had hoped," she said." You look very nice in those clothes, Talon. You should have them a long time.

Ed watched but said nothing until the table had been set and the food served.

"So how you coming with the horses?" He asked.

"They're good enough," said Talon." They will need rode a good bit but they're gentle, and the bay is already picking up on neck reining. The sorrel will still need some work on that, but she don't mind being rode, it don't seem."

"That's good then," said Ed. "Guess that means you will be on your way soon."

"In the morning I think. Don't want to seem ungrateful, but I have done about all I can with the horses and now that Janice has finished, it seems best to go."

He was sure that Ed would be glad to see him off. One less thing to worry about. He studied Ed a lot. Tried to read his face, and often could see that he was thinking a lot more than he was saying. He had not wanted Talon there in the first place but failed at stopping it. Talon was pretty sure that Ed had pondered why himself.

If he only knew, thought Talon.

"Well I was thinking about that," said Janice. "We should take the wagon in to Wolf Creek with Talon. I need to get fabric and drop some dresses off, and it would be a good way to see him off."

"I don't have time for no joy ride into town," said Ed. "I got more to do than gets done as it is. If Talon here hadn't worked them horses for me they might of died of old age before I got to em."

Janice didn't appear much moved by Ed not wanting to go. They were finishing eating when Janice decided that Ed had thought on the idea long enough. She knew him well.

"Are you sure you don't have anything you need in town, Ed?" she asked.

She was trying not to get pushy. Talon thought he could see storm clouds rolling in and was about to excuse himself when Lacey rose and picked up a few dishes.

"I have a personal matter to attend to," she said. "Please excuse me."

By personal matter, what she had meant was she needed to visit the little brown shack out back. Janice nodded and smiled. Lacey left the cabin. Talon would have left also but he wasn't sure if he should follow too close to Lacey. Ed was a suspicious man and he didn't need any trouble this close to trail time.

"I guess I could use some oats for the horses," Ed said. "Maybe should get some chicken feed as well. They don't do so well on just barley."

"Fine," said Janice. She was much happier sounding now. "This is good. We can all ride together in the morning."

"Oh Talon," she added. "If you bring your new clothes back over to me tonight, I will wrap them in a clean linen for travel. I have a lot of it."

"I will," said Talon.

Outside, Talon stopped on the porch and admired his new clothes again. He wished once more that Red Earth and Falling Water could see him now. *Fred Follows The Horses would be very proud for me,* he thought to himself. He missed him the most, but that was a life-time away now. He was on his way and doing well.

The last of the light had faded into sullen dark-ness when Talon reached the barn. He felt for the horse hair and discovered it was not tied to the door any longer. For a moment he tried to remember if he had tied it back or in his excitement could he have overlooked it. As he let the hair fall Lacey's voice came from inside his room.

"You may as well come in," she said. I know you're there. I saw you leave the cabin from your little window."

Talon's heart skipped a beat. Inside, he wouldn't be able to see well enough without the lamp to even know if she was dressed or not, and knowing Lacey, she might not be. He pushed the door open slowly.

"Come on in," she said. "We wouldn't want any-one to see you would we?"

"Lacey," said Talon. "What are you doing in my room?"

"We need to talk Talon."

"If your dad…" Talon said.

She interrupted him, "Never mind him," she said. "He don't matter anymore. I'm going with you."

"No you're not," said Talon. The words flew from him like a frightened bird. He hadn't meant to say it like that, but her words had knocked the mental wind out of him and he spoke before he could catch himself.

"I mean you can't. I can't let you. I don't want you to go with me. I have come to like traveling alone."

"Well that don't matter either," she informed him. "I'm coming anyway. If you don't let me then I will just follow you."

Talon tried to think what he should do. She was obviously not concerned that her father might miss her and come looking. Then it dawned on him that she might have that base covered. There was the chance that Janice already knew where she was. That wouldn't surprise him, but then there was Lacey herself. She seemed to have made up her mind.

Maybe I could outride her, thought Talon. It

wouldn't be easy but she wasn't used to long days on horseback, but if he did, she would be left out there somewhere alone. He doubted she knew the first thing about how to find shelter or food on the trail. It would be as good as killing her himself.

She's bluffing, he thought. *That's it. She knows she can't make it, and she's sure I won't leave her to rot either. No matter,* thought Talon. He knew he couldn't take her and if she wasn't bluffing... *Well,* thought Talon, *that's not my call.*

In a way, he understood her position. Anyone with a brain might feel like they were living in a place where they were not really wanted. It wouldn't take much of that to be enough for anyone. Even Ed wasn't enough for her. He was gone all day, and straight to bed at night.

He could see how the white culture was so good at building towns and large herds. They simply ignored all else until they were dead and one of their sons took over and did the same thing. *How sad,* thought Talon. *They don't even know each other. The only one who truly makes her feel loved don't hardly exist. When he is here it's a battle zone.*

Someday, thought Talon, *the white culture will fall to pieces. They are a people who cannot be content. It's not easy even for the Lakota, but we do know our own, and the time spent with them is life to us. How different are these two cultures? I am challenging all of the earth and even the spirits of the spirit house to have what they are leaving behind in their race to nowhere.*

"I think you are a good person," Said Talon, "and I don't want any hard feelings, but I can't take you with me. If you follow me, that would be your call but I will not share my camp with you. Your father would spend the rest of his life tracking you down and shoot me as sure as I'm standing here."

"Maybe so," said Lacey, "but that's not going to stop me. I have had all of this place I want, and a whole lot more. I will never have a life here. A woman needs to be in a place where there are people to meet."

"I don't blame you," said Talon. He knew there

was a lot more to it than that, but there was nothing he could do about it. He heard the rustle of her dress as she rose from the bed. An instant later, she pushed past him and crossed the barnyard without looking back.

Talon hurriedly dressed and returned the clothes to Janice. Sleep came hard for Talon that night, but at least the trail waited for him in the morning and he took comfort in that.

Janice stood by the work table and listened to Ed dress for bed. She had hoped that Talon was her doorway out, but that didn't look like it was going to happen. She didn't hate Lacey, in fact, a part of her loved Lacey, but she was a restless woman. She would never have chosen this life in the first place if not for Lacey.

Ed was as good a man as they came, but he wouldn't have been her choice either, not under any other circumstances. She needed him. Not for a husband though, for a daddy. What she knew she could never tell. It would kill Ed if he ever knew. Lacey was not his. Still, there was one more thing Talon might be able to do for her. One little deed left. She folded the special gift, wrapped it into the clothes bundle with Talon's clothes and bound them tight.

CHAPTER 7

BRODIE BUCKHART

Brodie Buckhart was a man Talon had never met, or ever would, but Brodie Buckhart was about to play a part in Talon's life that would change a great many things, not all of them to the good. Brodie had left the big city of Buffalo, Wyoming a few days earlier on the stage home. He was dressed like a rich man, and that for good reason. Brodie was the son of a prominent rancher fifteen miles south of the town of Wolf Creek.

His father had money, but he wasn't loose with it, not even for Brodie. His father's name was Lance, and Lance had decided that Brodie should have to work for what he got like anyone else. He paid him more than the other hands, but he paid him by the month like any other ranch hand.

Brodie had left home a couple weeks earlier, with the total of two months pay in his pocket, for the big city. He had never seen the city before and he had decided it was time.

The big city, he discovered, was big indeed. There were automobiles there. They were amazing to him, and he sat for two hours on a street corner bench just to watch them go by.

They didn't smell good, and they were noisy, but they were remarkable to him. He also saw finer horses there than he had ever seen in his life before. Fine horses hitched to fine little two-wheeled carts all upholstered in leather. In those little carts were fine women and men, all dressed in far nicer clothes than he even knew existed.

They had electric lights there, and on every street corner was a lamp on a pole that lit the walk all night long.

All the shops were highly attractive, as were all the fine carts and people. Even the trail hands seemed more sophisticated. They stood around a lot and stared as well. The shops were remarkable. There were things there that little old Wolf Creek would never know. He had made up his mind to change a little of that and set out to find some of those fine clothes for himself.

Wolf Creek was a small town, and compared to Buffalo it amounted to very little. Mostly one street that ran down the center of town, and four shorter streets that crossed it where shops and houses were.

On Main Street, the first thing you saw as you entered from the east, was the sheriff's office. Domingo Wells was the town sheriff. His only deputy was a short, stout man whose name was Axle Ford.

Domingo was an average height man with broad shoulders and fast hands. He had gotten the job because of the fast hands. Axle was better with a rifle but was no stranger to a pistol himself. His best selling point was that he was fearless. Not careless, but fearless. He had discovered somewhere in his past that fear was a choice. He chose not to. He was one of those people you meet now and again that don't need to boast. They don't make excuses either, they just get things done.

Domingo and Axle had become good friends over the past five years of service to Wolf Creek. They understood each other. Axle wasn't stupid, far from it. It was, however, Domingo who was the working brains. He understood people. He could peg a liar from across the street and he knew bad blood when he saw it. He was also the more level-headed of the two. Axle had very little patience for ignorance in any form. His idea for leading such people was to break their nose. Or if not, then shoot em down. He wasn't cold blooded, he just had no patience with stupid people. To govern the city needed them both.

The town of Wolf Creek was a gathering place for ranchers and wanderers alike. The most important thing a sheriff needed to do there was keep the peace between the cowboys and the Indians. They got along most of the time, as long as nobody started drinking. That happened about every night.

The stage stop was the next business, on the same side of the street as the sheriff's office. Domingo was on the boardwalk, taking in the afternoon sun, when the stage pulled up and let Brodie Buckhart out. He watched as Brodie made his way down the street and around the corner with his bag in his hand.

Brodie wasn't a large man, but he was large enough. Domingo had arrested him on more than one occasion for fighting. He liked to push the local Indians around when he got to drinking. They were usually smaller than he was and were easy targets. It's a long dry ride from Buffalo and Domingo figured he knew where Brodie would stop next.

"Axle," he called through the open office door. Axle stepped out onto the boardwalk.

"Just so you know," said Domingo. "Brodie Buckhart just got back, and he's wearing more money than you or I make in a couple months. Try and guess where he is likely headed."

"Well," said Axle, "there is the barber. Was he nice and shaved?"

"Yep"

"Might be a good thing then, cause if he's headed where I expect he is, that being shaved might save the undertaker a little trouble."

"How so? I don't know any Indians that fast with a gun."

"Me neither," said Axle." But I just came from down there at Lady Dandy's, and there is a whole new supply of Indians down there, and some I ain't never seen before."

Domingo tipped his hat up and looked up at Axle.

"Maybe we ought to get a shotgun or two loaded and ready, in that case," said Domingo.

Just past the stage stop was a motel. Fixed to the corner of it was a banner that stretched across Main Street from side to side. It was at the corner of the first crossing street in town. The banner read "Lady Dandy's Saloon" and an arrow pointed up that street to the north.

Beyond the banner, the rest of the town was laid out like you might expect. There was a dress shop where Janice sold her well-made clothes. There was a small bank and a collection of other businesses that made up the rest of the town. One of those businesses was the trading post of Owen Underhill.

The trading post was the only grocery store in town and also the post office. The front of the post was made of a large window that was divided up into little squares of glass. It exposed the street for the entire front of the store. On the boardwalk in front of his shop were a couple of Army surplus saddles with new head rigs draped over the saddle horns. They were high-backed and well-made saddles and were unused.

The undertaker had a shop just beyond the trading post and after that was a wood shop that among other things, made the caskets for the undertaker.

Neither one did much business. In spite of a lot of drunken fist fights, it was a rare thing for anyone to get themselves killed.

Brodie made for the town stable to retrieve the horse he had left there for safe keeping while he was away.

Between him and the stable was Lady Dandy's saloon. Brodie thought it would be a fun thing to do, to stop in and strut around a little. It would be a long ride home, and a dry one. Anyway, the day was half gone already and the moon would be full tonight, so, no point to getting into a hurry now.

That decision turned out to be one of those little-noticed things that determines everything. It was the decision that would prove in the end to be fatal.

The saloon was already starting to come to life when he arrived. He looked around and took mental notice of all the faces that he might know. There were more than a few. He walked hard on his way to the bar. Any harder and he would have been stomping.

It pleased him to see that a number of locals were noticing his new clothes and hat, especially his boots. They were riding boots but were made strong for working in as well. There wasn't anything especially fancy about the look of them except that they were obviously very well made, of exceptionally good leather.

The builder of the boots had stitched a design across the toe in red thread, whose only purpose was to decorate the boot. It did a nice job of that, but that was the only thing about the boots that was not functional by design.

The heel was a tapered design, and tall enough to stop one's foot from slipping through the stirrups. The toe was more rounded than most riding boots. That made them more comfortable to wear for other kinds of work. The tops were twelve inches high. They also had very little dressy stitching. What they amounted to, were very nice looking work boots. They were brand new and anyone could tell at a glance.

Brodie took his new hat off when he reached the

bar and spun it in his hands a couple times, admiring it before he ordered his beer. Everyone he knew in the place was looking at him, especially the ever-present Indians that sat at a table in the corner. They watched him for a little while, and then went back to their drinks and cards.

Time drifted by unnoticed, and the night was closing in. Brodie hadn't meant to stay so long. He was expected at home that night, but the bar had been full of other cowboys from nearby ranches, and his trip to the big city was of interest to most of them.

In the course of time, he began to notice the Indians at the corner table. Some of them he remembered, from having beat them up in past fights. Tonight he noticed more than usual, and some of them looked like they were of tribes he hadn't seen before, or if he did, he couldn't remember where.

He was in the right mood for a fight, but he thought better of it. There were more than usual, and not enough cowboys to cover his back if need be, but more than that, he was dressed in the best clothes he had ever even seen and wanted to look good when he got home. Not that anyone would be awake by then to notice, but they would see them sooner or later, and having blood on them or getting them torn would simply not do at all.

Axle waited just inside the bar door. He had slipped in earlier in the evening and waited. The trouble he expected never came, but he had noticed the Indians that afternoon. It was like they were waiting for something or perhaps planning something. He had seen plenty of nights when there were a lot of Indians in town and they were just taking care of business. This could be just that and nothing more, but he had learned not to take chances. If something did go south down at Dandy's, it could result in all-out war.

More and more Indians had been coming to town these days, as they became more accustomed to the white culture and that meant clashes, but these Indians seemed quiet. *Too quiet,* he thought. They talked among themselves a lot in hushed tones, but he was used to that. They had few white friends and none that he knew they confided in.

There was no way they could have known Brodie was going to be there. If they were looking for someone else he couldn't figure who. They didn't seem to be troubled about anything and stayed to themselves. Better for everyone, thought Axle.

Brodie left the bar that night more drunk than not and half-staggered down the street to the stable. He paid up and left town for home.

CHAPTER 8

SADDLE UP AND RIDE

Talon was packed before daylight. The cabin had come to life as well. A lamp shone out through the front window. He stood at the edge of the corral where he had tied his horses and waited for day.

The bay walked over to where he was and lifted her head over the rail. At first, he thought she was looking for a treat. When she brushed him with her head he realized she was just saying hi. She was a good horse. He was glad he had time to say goodbye to her.

He had thought he might ride out in the night to avoid any problem with Lacey and he still wished he had. The only reason he chose not to was the clothes. Janice still had them inside.

A quiet breeze moved across the corral and carried the smell of blooming sage and pine. The owl drifted by silently as the first light of day began to fill the sky, and a nighthawk began to call.

Any time now, thought Talon, and there it was right on cue, the rooster crowed. The day had begun. The air was cool and clean, but he could already feel the promise of heat from the rising sun. He turned to look at the cabin, just as the door opened and Lacey stepped out onto the porch. She saw that he was looking at her and waved him in for breakfast.

The air in the cabin seemed filled with excitement and smelled of bread and bacon. The sewing machine had been covered with a clean linen cloth and beside it on the table was a bundle also wrapped in linen.

"So," said Janice, "big day ahead."

"Yep," Ed said, and went back to eating.

"You put plenty of feed out for the chickens?" Janice asked Lacey.

"Plenty," said Lacey.

"Well then," said Janice, "we can just load the wagon and be on our way. Will you want your clothes with you Talon, or should we keep them in the wagon till we get to town?

"Best if I pack them right off," said Talon.

"I thought so," she said. "They are in that bundle over there. I packed some food for you as well. You'll make better time if you have a bit of a grubstake."

"That's very nice of you," said Talon. He hadn't thought of food. He was thinking of the trail and just wanted to get moving. Breakfast went quicker than usual, and Ed left the cabin before Talon finished.

"By the way, Talon," said Janice." I packed a small surprise for you with your clothes. It isn't much but it was something I've had for a while, and no one here will ever wear it. I know you will like it, but it's for the trail so you must promise to not look until you are well on your way. I don't want you to try and not take it. You have been a very nice guest. I just wanted you to have something to remember us by. You will wait to unwrap it won't you?"

"Yes Ma'am," said Talon. "I promise."

It was mid-afternoon when the Clanton party started down the main street of Wolf Creek. The sidewalks were busy and people were everywhere. A freight wagon met them with a four-horse team and passed on their left. Talon watched as it passed. The driver had a shotgun rider sitting next to him on the seat. When it passed, Talon could see the rest of the town. The Clanton wagon pulled up at the little hotel and tied off at the rail.

"Well," said Ed, "this is it." He stepped down from the wagon. We will stay in town tonight and ride back in the morning."

Talon was still mounted and Ed reached up and shook his hand.

"Guess you will want to be on your way. It's been good to know you."

"Yes sir," said Talon.

He didn't know what else to say. He turned to wave goodbye to Janice and Lacey.

"You promise now," said Janice, "you won't open it till you get out on the trail."

"I promise," he said.

Lacey tried to smile but he could see that she was not happy. He waved goodbye and turned the paint west. The bundle Janice had given him was in the bottom of his pack. He thought about it as he set out down the street. He turned to look one more time at the Clantons. Lacey was the last to leave the wagon. She was getting her bag and she was watching him leave. He waved again and then turned back to his freedom.

He had been watching the shops drift by and was in high spirits. He had expected people to think it odd that there was an Indian in town, but no one even looked up from what they were doing. It didn't take long to see why. Looking around he saw that he was not alone. There were other Indians ahead of him. Not in great number, but they were there.

Some of the nations he recognized. He thought he might know some of the others but couldn't be sure. He was looking up the street and waiting for the last building to start to disappear behind him when he heard a small bell. It was to his right and caught his attention. When he looked he saw saddles. A man had just left the shop where the saddles were and the door had been fixed to a small bell to warn of a customer coming in. Above the door were the words Trading Post.

He stopped and looked closer at the saddles. They were on saddle trees just in front of a large window that looked into the store. Inside the store was a table that had been pushed up against the window. Around the table were three men drinking coffee and watching the street as if they had nothing else to do. Behind the men were shelves of food and other tack. It reminded him that he still had one dollar in his pocket. Janice had packed him some food, but he had no idea what, and he liked the idea of having a few cans of beans and pork.

That was another thing the white culture had brought that he liked, canned food, especially beans and pork. He also liked fruit in the cans. Some of the fruits were new to him, like peaches, and apricots.

What he really wanted to do was look closer at the saddles. He tied off at the hitching rail and made for the door. On the way, he stopped and looked the saddles over. Not wanting to draw undue attention, he gave them a quick once over and went on into the store.

The store was quiet except for the men's conversation at the table.

"Mornin", said the man behind the counter. It was Owen Underhill. "What can I help you with?"

Talon looked around the store. "You got any beans in cans?" He asked.

"Sure I do," said Owen. "Third isle on the left."

Talon found the beans and had enough to buy more than he wanted to carry. He chose five cans.

"Fine horse you got there," said Owen.

He was looking at the paint through the window in the door of the shop. Talon put the armload of cans up on the counter.

"Yes sir," he said. "You got peaches in cans too?"

"Sure I do," said Owen. "Just down a little from where you found the beans. "Judgin from here, I'd say you could use a nice saddle for that horse."

Talon put the dollar up onto the counter and Owen counted him back a few cents change.

"As you must have noticed, I got a few nice ones out on the walk. Surplus from the Army, cheap. I could sell you one of them saddles for no more'n twenty dollars. They all come with the head rig that goes with them. Snaffle bits. Can't do better an that, can ya?"

Talon looked out at the saddles. He noticed on his way in that the one on the end looked about the right size for him but he hadn't studied it long. He figured them to be worth more than he had and passed.

"No thanks," Said Talon, "I don't have that much money."

"Well, what you got to trade then?" Asked Owen." You got any guns?"

For a moment Talon thought of the 45-70 on the

packhorse. He could trade that, but he worried that he might need it. The trail could be a dangerous place. It made him wish he had more than just one round of ammunition for it, but that would have to do.

He was about to say no when it hit him. He looked into Owen's eyes. Owen didn't look like the kind of man you could easily fool. *Still,* he thought, *what have I got to lose?* Talon smiled. He reached up and pulled the three feathers from his hair and held them out to Owen.

"Feathers?" Said Owen

"Eagle feathers," said Talon.

Owen laughed. "You must be nuts," he said.

The men at the table stopped talking to listen. One of them chuckled a little.

"Come on kid," said Owen, "you ain't simple enough to think I would trade you a saddle for feathers." Talon laid the feathers on the counter. "You can keep your feathers," said Owen.

"What feathers?" asked Talon."

Owen looked a little puzzled. "Why them three

feathers you put on the counter there."

Talon looked down at the feathers. "You mean these four feathers on the counter? These ain't just feathers, these are eagle's feathers."

"Ya, whatever kid, ain't interested."

"These are nice ones. You ain't trying to cheat me are you?"

"Cheat ya?" asked Owen.

"You trying to get one feather for free."

Owen looked confused. The men at the table were starting to laugh a little louder. Owen smiled and laughed along a little.

"You said three, I offered you four. Not three."

Owen looked at the feathers again.

"Three kid, there's just three."

"You run a store and you can't count," said Talon. "How do you stay in business like that?"

Owen looked again at the three feathers. He took what Talon had said for an insult, an insult from a kid no less.

"I can count just fine, kid." He was starting to feel

a little embarrassed. He looked over at the table.

"You better look out," one of the men at the table said. "That kid could make you look pretty bad if it turns out there is four."

The feathers were laying side by side and easy to see. Owen was certain enough but the thought that there was another one under one of the others occurred to him. He lifted each one and looked carefully at them. He looked up at Talon and was starting to wonder what he might be up to.

"How many years schooling you got boy? You can't count to three."

Talon looked over to the table where the other men were. "One of you guys might have more than first grade learning over there? Maybe you could come count these feathers for this fella. He can't get past three."

One of the men started to get up. Owen took him for serious.

"Bailey!" Said Owen. "You don't think I can count either? You just keep your seat over there. I can handle this just fine."

He looked back at Talon. "Now look kid," he said. "I don't know what you are up to, but there ain't but three feathers on that countertop and I ain't trading no saddle for em." He was sounding a little frustrated.

Bailey walked over and looked at the feathers himself. He started to reach out to inspect them but Talon put up his hand to stop him. When he did a red flag popped up in Owen's mind. He began to doubt what he was seeing. He looked at the feathers with careful scrutiny.

"How many you see Bailey?" Owen asked. He was beginning to wonder.

"Just three," said Bailey.

He was looking at them more carefully now himself.

"Just three?" Talon asked.

He looked into Owen's eyes again. "You sure?"

Owen looked at Bailey and smiled. "Ya, I'm sure kid," he said and stepped back from the counter a little. He crossed his arms and stood looking at Talon.

"How sure are you?" Talon asked. "You could be wrong, you know. There could be four feathers. If you ain't wrong, you going to give me one of those saddles?"

Talon tried to look a little indignant and stood up as straight as he could. Owen looked at Bailey again.

"Ya kid, I'm that sure."

Talon smiled and picked up the feathers. Then he gathered his canned goods and made for the door.

"Thank you," he called over his shoulder.

He had the saddle and was hurriedly putting it on the paint before Owen realized what had happened.

"Wait," said Owen." Did he say if you ain't wrong?"

The trading post exploded with laughter.

"Well I'll be hanged," said Owen.

179

He wasn't sure what he should do. It was a more or less honest deal, just like the ones he liked the best.

Talon had his three feathers. He had won a saddle but he wasn't sure how strong the deal was. He saddled up and hit the trail before anyone could change their mind. The laughter faded away behind him as he made for the other end of town with his canned goods and a nice new saddle.

Janice Clanton watched Talon saddle his horse from the window in the motel room. He had come out of the store and stuffed something into the panniers on the packhorse. Then he all but ran back up onto the boardwalk and snatched one of the saddles off its tree out front and tossed it up onto his horse. Then he bounced into it without using the stirrups and headed out at a fast canter.

Imagine that, she thought to herself. As she watched Talon leave, Owen Underhill and his brother Bailey had come out of the shop with two other men she didn't recognize. They were laughing. One of the men said something to Owen and then slapped him on the back and laughed some more. When Talon was gone, they went back into the shop. As the door closed behind them, Janice's curiosity flamed up like a fuel fire. She would have to check that out, she told herself. Tomorrow, in the morning; it could wait till then.

CHAPTER 9

JR BAD WATER

On the same day that Talon entered the town of Wolf Creek, at around three that morning, a rifle shot rang out ten miles away.

Brodie Buckhart had been riding home. He was about five miles short of the ranch, and still pretty drunk, but he knew where he was. It was a narrow part of the road that bottlenecked between two ridges. He never heard the shot that killed him.

By six that morning Lance Buckhart was getting worried. Brodie was late. He knew when the stage should have gotten to Wolf Creek and he allowed time for Brodie to get ready and leave town.

That should of meant that Brodie would be home the night before. He reasoned that he might of stayed in town, but that would mean renting a room. He rejected the idea and sent a couple buckaroos to look for him. They came back in, on frothed up horses, at a dead run.

"Better get the boss," one of them called out to one of the hands on the porch of the bunkhouse. "We got trouble, and plenty of it."

Crew boss for the Buckhart ranch was a man named Billy Dean. He was about to head to the cook shack for breakfast when the buckaroos rode up.

"What kind of trouble?" He wanted to know.

"It's Brodie! Somebody shot him. He's dead!"

"Someone shot Brodie! Who the Sam hill would shoot Brodie?"

"Can't tell, but I can tell you they left with his boots and hat on a barefoot horse."

Billy kicked the bunkhouse door open with the toe of his boot. "Saddle up," he yelled. "I want

184

every man on this spread saddled up and ready to ride in five minutes."

Lance had heard from the other buckaroo, but couldn't believe his ears. Brodie was rowdy. In fact, he was more than rowdy, he was a bit of a bully, but he hadn't ever done anything Lance knew of worth killing him over.

He was torn between panic and remorse as he all but ran from the main house headed for the barn. One of the ranch hands already had his horse mostly saddled and helped him finish, and he mounted up.

He set out hard and was joined by the entire crew before he reached the yard gate. They found Brodie where the Buckaroos had left him. He was sure enough dead, alright. Lance couldn't believe his eyes. Someone had shot him out of his saddle.

The bullet had entered from the back and blew most of his heart out. He never knew what hit him. His horse stood a few yards away. Drying blood was on the saddle and in the mane hair of the horse.

Lance knelt down next to Brodie and brushed

the hair from his eyes. He let his eyes drift down Brodie's body to his feet. Shot for his boots? There had to be more to it than that. He would find that out later. For now, Brodie was dead and nothing could change that.

"Take him home," he said in a quiet voice. "Keep him cool. You can spread a table in the cellar."

Lance couldn't watch as two of the buckaroos started to lift Brodie to his horse. He turned away fighting tears. On the ground, a few feet away, he saw barefoot horse tracks. The instant he saw them, rage consumed his mind. He could never talk to Brodie again, but he could find the coward that had killed him, and God help that man when he found him.

The fight that ended in the death of Brodie Buckhart started the year before. A Sioux Indian, new to town, had wandered in from the Pine Ridge country, south and west of Wolf Creek. He was shorter than Brodie but stout and about ten years older than Brodie. The Sioux's name was JR Bad Water.

He was drinking at Dandy's place. Brodie was there that night and started a fight with an Indian a little younger than him and a head shorter.

JR was a drinking man and a bar room brawler most of his adult life and took it personal that Brodie was trying to goad the smaller man into a fight. It didn't take much to put JR on the warpath. He was drunk. He thought that Brodie was just as drunk, and stepped into the fight, as much because he wanted to, as for any other reason. Brodie was not drunk enough, and beat JR down. Once on the floor, he put his boots to him.

It took JR a month to heal up, but it didn't stop him. When he was ready, he returned to Dandy's looking for trouble with Brodie and found it. Brodie was there about any Friday or Saturday night.

That fight was a whole lot different than the first.

JR waited until he thought Brodie was drunk enough and lit into him nearly sober. The fight had lasted about twenty minutes before Brodie started showing signs of wearing out. He was guarding a lot and missing his mark about half the time.

JR was winning, and he knew he was. He planted a hard haymaker to the side of Brodie's head and watched him bounce off the bar and hit the floor. That was the last thing he saw. One of Brodie's buddies slammed him in the side of the head with a full bottle of whiskey and Brodie put the boots to him again.

JR knew what everyone else knew, Brodie had lost the fight. He figured that losing the fight might slow Brodie down a little, and even though he needed another month to heal up, he felt a little better about it this time.

Years of bar fighting had hardened JR to brutal wounds and he wore them well, but this one had not quite healed the night Brodie rode in from Buffalo and made his way down to Lady Dandy's saloon. JR watched him come in. He had been there drinking and was already getting a little wild-eyed when Brodie entered.

He had chosen a table opposite the other Indians, so as not to draw attention to himself. He had no way of knowing that Brodie would be there that night, or any other for that part, but he wasn't in a mood for cards, and wanted to drink alone. Besides that, the table he chose was close to the back door and he never knew when that might come in handy.

Brodie was busy with tall talk and whiskey, and never saw JR. He had noticed the other Indians, but they were no threat.

The longer Brodie strutted and talked, the more it galled JR. He studied the new boots and hat and wanted to stain Brodie's new jacket with his own blood in a very bad way. Brodie, as usual, had a lot of backup, and JR had already seen what that meant. His perception of Brodie was that he was a spoiled little rich kid, living privileged, who had never seen a hungry day in his life. That thought made things all the more painful. His perception didn't miss the truth by much.

That was another thing that he hated about Brodie. If he had been a common buckaroo, the other cowboys would not have been as eager to back him up. He knew he could whip Brodie, and the longer he watched him the drunker he got. He kept looking at Brodie's boots.

In the course of time, he decided he wanted them and he thought he knew how he could get them. *Get Brodie too,* he thought.

An hour before Brodie left the saloon, JR was on the trail to the Buckhart Ranch. He knew the country as well as any man and waited in the little canyon short of the ranch. He chose the place for all the right reasons. Lots of cover close to the trail was the first. It was a full moon night. The shadows were long and dark in the little canyon, and there were juniper trees a plenty to hide a horse close by for a quick escape.

He had found a large rock about the size of a wagon and settled in behind it. By the time Brodie arrived at the spot, JR was almost asleep. The whiskey was still heavy in his blood and the night was warm.

Brodie rode his horse at walking pace. He was still pretty plowed himself. He might of heard JR stagger out from behind the rock if he had been sober, but if pigs had wings they could fly.

At first, JR had not planned to shoot Brodie. His plan was to confront him in a place where he would not have his constant backup boys, but he realized, as Brodie got closer, that he was much too drunk to win a fight with a woman, much less a seasoned fighter.

Brodie had passed by fifty feet or so before the rage in JR started getting out of control. He had cheated himself out of his one opportunity to even the score.

He stumbled from his hiding place and leveled the 30-30 rifle at Brodie's back. He didn't bother trying to aim. He didn't care.

If he missed, Brodie would have no choice but to run, and for the moment watching him run back to Daddy would have to do. If he didn't miss, that was okay too. He held the rifle in both hands and pulled the trigger. He didn't miss.

Lance and six of his men set out on the tracks of the barefoot pony. JR had gone back up the canyon to where it began and headed west on a path that stayed clear of the main road headed west out of Wolf Creek. He wasn't sure how long it would take for the Buckhart boys to start missing Brodie.

He figured even after they found him, they would have to go to Wolf Creek for the sheriff. It might take a day to round up a posse. That might mean two days with luck. By then, he would be way ahead and making tracks. Figuring he had a little time, he wasn't trying to run yet. He was still too drunk.

Twice, one of the oversized boots had slipped off and he had to stop to get it back. On two other occasions, he fell off his horse trying to grab a boot that was coming off. Every time he looked down, the ground started spinning. It made travel hard, but he stayed with it as long as he could. He was gradually getting more sober, so he moved a little faster. He wasn't sure how far he had gone, but it felt like a good distance. It was around two in the afternoon when he stopped to rest. He was feeling a little sick.

Lance was thinking just the opposite. He expected to be in the saddle for a couple days. He would have stayed a couple months if need be. The six men he had with him were running on boiling blood as well.

The trail JR left was easy to find, and they were on him with little effort. JR lay half asleep in the shade of the tree when he heard the horses coming. They were on his trail. He was not near the road so there was no other reason for them to be there. In a panic, he fought his way back up onto his horse, losing one of the boots in the process. He dug his heels into the pony and tried for the dense cover of the hillside behind him.

One of the cowboys caught a glimpse of him as he passed between two of the large juniper trees. "There he goes," he yelled and fired a wild shot in JR's direction.

"Don't shoot him!" yelled Lance. "I want him to hang."

The chase was short. JR couldn't stay on his horse and he soon fell. The horse stopped. JR didn't. The hill was steep, and he slid about sixty feet down and stopped up against a dead cottonwood tree near a small spring. His 30-30 slipped from his hands and slid across the damp green grass, then into the little pond created by the spring and sank partly into the mud.

Lance was off his horse and on the ground with JR in one leap. There was yelling and fighting as JR tried a weak defense with a knife. Lance met him with the butt of his rifle in the face and the knife was lost in the grass. He was still alive when the rope went tight. JR died without a trial, but he died as he always would have. It was only a matter of time. He hadn't stopped swinging when Lance turned his men back toward the Buckhart Ranch. The rage and heartbreak would haunt him to his grave, but the knowledge that JR ended at his hand would always be some little comfort.

"One of you boys get to town," he said. "You go tell Wells about my boy, then get back to the ranch."

A tall man named Jack Lambert volunteered. He looked one more time at JR, who was just stopping his swing, and turned toward town at a fast trot.

Chapter 10

The Hanging Man's Boots

About the time the rope went tight, Talon was just leaving Wolf Creek. The deal he had made on the saddle was as good as any other gambling deal. That was part of the reason he was in a hurry. He had never met Owen Underhill and had no way to know how he might take it. Some people, he knew, were not good losers and he didn't need reminded that he was an Indian.

He left town and made tracks for the north and west on a trail that stayed clear of the main road. He stayed close enough to the main road to keep an eye on it, in case he was followed. Any place there was high ground above the road he chose it. It slowed him down a little, but not so much to be concerned. Being able to watch his back trail was more important.

About an hour into the ride he stopped to check the saddle. He had saddled his horse in a hurry and couldn't be sure he had not trapped some of the tie down laces under the saddle or left a fold in the blanket. He was putting the saddle back on the horse and ready to tighten the cinch, when a dust trail on the main road caught his attention.

A cowboy on a long-legged horse was moving at a fast canter toward town. Talon was far enough away not to see much else. It looked like the horse was lathered up and had been pushing hard. He watched as the cowboy passed and then finished his own work with the saddle. He thought it odd that the cowboy was in such a hurry, but put it out of his mind. He had enough to worry about.

The trail he was on was a game trail that came and went. Talon wasn't familiar with the area but he was sure he needed to stay near the road until he came to a place where the road crossed two creeks right before they merged into one deeper one.

He had learned of the place from Ed Clanton. It was all he knew. Ed had told him that the road headed south from there and he would do well to take to the trees and stay more north. If he wandered too far west from there, he would run into a place called the badlands. He never said why they called them that. He never told him how far it was either. The day was fading, and Talon wondered if he would make it to the crossing before dark.

He was watching the trail and keeping the sun in front of him when the trail suddenly turned and headed south. He followed a short way to see if it turned again. It didn't, so he corrected to the west again. He had gone less than a hundred yards when he found why the trail had changed. There was a road in front of him. It caught him by surprise. It was at a place where the road cut through thick timber and was hid from view.

Had he been more familiar with the area he would have known that he was about to cross the road to the Buckhart Ranch. It was not a much-used road but it had seen horse traffic that day. Talon sat still a few yards from the road in a willow thicket. He waited to see if he was alone or if someone might be on the road. He wanted to cross unseen, if possible.

He couldn't see much and all he could hear was the light wind in the trees. A small bird fluttered between the trees, and a jack rabbit crossed the road farther up. He heard it scatter a little sand as it bounced off the other side and back into the trees.

He was good at listening. It wasn't something most people seemed to know you could get good at. It took practice to really hear what was going on around him in his younger days. What he discovered was that you needed to hear all there was to hear, then isolate every sound until it could be identified. Wind in the grass and trees made things a little harder to hear, but practice had taught him how. He waited and listened intently and then crossed and hurried off into the trees on the other side.

Soon after, he picked up another game trail and began working it farther west. He lost track of time, watching for game and enjoying the evening. It may have been an hour or even two before things changed. He was moving along looking for a camp spot. The trail had begun to climb and wander farther from the main road.

He was thinking of Lacey Clanton, worried that she might actually try to follow him. He was glad he had chosen to stay off the roads. She would have to go home, he figured, and that would mean she couldn't even start out until she was able to get the bay. He was thinking she would be too far behind by then.

A movement in the trees ahead caught his attention and he put her out of his mind. Whatever it was, had stopped. Talon pulled up and froze. Whatever it was, he didn't think it saw him. It was too far away. It didn't seem to be going anywhere, so he moved a little closer. A few steps later he could see it plainly. It was a horse. It had a head rig on, but nothing else.

Talon waited to see if it was alone or if its rider was someplace near.

The horse was cropping grass and seemed unconcerned as he approached. He rode up to where it was standing. The only tracks on the trail were the tracks of the horse. He looked for man tracks off trail but the hill was steep. No logical person would be off the trail. He brushed past the horse's rump as he passed. Still unconcerned, it kept with the grass so Talon caught up the reigns and put the horse in tow. The trail was narrow, and he was forced to lengthen the lead rope on his packhorse to make room between them for the lost horse.

A short time later, the trail rounded a small ridge in the trees and allowed a view of the hillside coming up. In the draw between, the trail dropped a little and then leveled off. It was here that Talon discovered more horse tracks. The horse he had found was barefooted. The horses that had left these tracks had shoes. Talon stopped to inspect the tracks. Five or six horses had come down the hillside fast.

The ground was chewed up like it had been plowed. It looked fresh. Moving slow, he rode silently around a large juniper tree at the edge of the trail. The next thing he saw stopped him in his tracks.

Along the side of the trail, and down the bank a short way lay a new boot. It was a nice one and the right size. Talon dismounted and picked it up. He thought about trying it on. It was an excellent boot, but it was only one. Besides that, he was getting a very bad feeling about the day. He climbed back up to his horse and moved forward.

The tracks for the barefoot horse left the trail and headed for deeper tree cover on the side of the hill. The rest stayed along the trail and then plummeted off downhill toward a large cottonwood tree.

Talon decided on the tracks that went down. Before he left the trail, he dismounted and tied his horses to the juniper. Pulling the 45-70 from his pack, he crept down the hill as carefully as possible. A few yards closer to the cottonwood tree a slight movement caught his eye.

He stopped and studied it. At first, it was hard to make out through the brush, but with a little study, he could see what it was. Someone was standing near the tree.

JR had a morbid sort of disgusted look on what was left of his face. Talon could only see his head from where he was. The rest was only a dark shadow in the willows by the spring.

Something looked strange about his face, not just the blood and bruises. There was something else. He wasn't moving like a man should. He was sort of swaying. Then he saw it. JR's neck was much too long for a healthy man and it had a noose around it.

After a moment of silence, Talon moved closer. JR was swinging at the end of the rope. His feet were about a yard off the ground and directly under them was the other boot.

Talon stood for a moment and stared. He had never seen a man that had been hanged before and wasn't sure what he should do. He thought of burying him.

He decided he would do well to leave things as he found them. He wouldn't want someone to think he had been involved. Anyway, JR was dead. What would it matter?

He was going to leave when he saw the hat. It was a new hat. It had fallen off when JR fell from his horse and the wind had carried it down the hill to the brush near the spring. It was too much to resist. Talon walked over and picked it up. When he tried it on it fit nicely. By that time, he was standing only a few feet from JR. *Why not,* thought Talon as he looked at the boot on the ground. He couldn't figure how an Indian could come up with enough money for the hat, much less the boots, but that didn't matter. The Indian was dead, and they were very nice boots. Talon reached down and picked the other boot up. It was a beautiful piece of work. Made with fine leather. *These boots and hat,* thought Talon, *will go just perfect with the rest of my new clothes.*

He looked up at JR. It was an ugly scene, and it was in a place that was well hidden. In a few weeks of summer heat the hanging man would be scattered bones, and the rope would be hanging alone from the tree.

Too bad for him, thought Talon. He brushed the dust from the boot and climbed back to his horses. After he got the rifle back into the panniers, he added the boots to his pack and tied them down with a short leather thong. Then he tied the flap closed and turned his attention to the horse JR had been riding.

It wasn't a bad looking horse, but the last thing he needed was to be mistaken for a horse thief. He removed the head rig and let it go free. The head rig was old and not in good shape. Talon tossed it down the bank, in the direction of the cottonwood tree. He heard it hit the ground in the underbrush somewhere below him and then mounted his horse.

The trail stayed more or less level in elevation for a long way after that and wound in and out of juniper and pine trees. The hill stayed rather steep and sun rays came and went. It rounded a large rock outcropping, with moss on it, and a little grass growing where it could find root space. The air was damp and cool, and the smell of the trees and wild roses, just beginning to bloom, drifted by. Except for the songbirds and a little breeze, the forest was silent. It was if nothing had ever happened.

A man was dead, maybe more than one, but the world did not seem to notice. No more than if a fox had killed a bird. It seemed natural to him. Men, he believed, thought much too highly of themselves most of the time. He felt an unease about the hanging man. In his spirit, he began to believe that he had not seen the end of that yet.

The sun was setting when Talon broke from the trees and began to follow a nice stream flowing from the Northwest. He might have found a place and crossed it, but he hoped it was one of the streams Ed had told him of.

After a half-mile or so, he came to the road and found that it was. From there, he went farther north through the trees and climbed up a ridge to the plateau on its top. From here he could see his back trail. He made a dry camp and rolled out his bed. Sleep did not come easy.

Chapter 11

Posse on His Trail

Jack Lambert arrived at the sheriff's office around six that evening. Axle Ford was at the desk.

"I need to see sheriff Wells," he told Axle.

"He's out back," said Axle. "Anything I can help you with?"

Domingo Wells came in before he could reply. He didn't know Jack Lambert, but he could see that he was in some sort of trouble, by the look on his face.

"Should I know you?" He asked.

Jack was pale as a ghost. "Name's Jack Lambert,

I work for the Buckhart. I figure you know them. Somebody's gone and killed Brodie. Shot him in the back."

Enough thinking for two hours passed through Domingo's mind in about the same number of seconds. He remembered seeing Brodie get off the stage. Then the words Axle said came back to mind, about the Indians in town. He hoped it wasn't connected.

"You see it?"

"No," said Jack." But I seen Brodie an I seen the man hang who done it."

Jack explained the day's events to Domingo. He then waited to see what the sheriff would do.

"You hanged him?" Asked Domingo.

"I was there. It was that Indian fella from Dandy's place. Him and Brodie been fighting days gone."

Domingo looked over at Axle. "Better start looking for a posse," Said Domingo.

"Why you need a posse?" Asked Jack. "We already hanged the man who done it."

"Well it sounds like you hanged someone, al-right," said Domingo. "If you happened to get the right someone, then all we need to deal with is the boys who done the hanging."

"It's the right one. He was wearing Brodie's boots."

"And you don't suppose that someone could have handed them boots off to someone else after the fight? Someone who wanted to send you a lookin for the wrong man?"

"Not likely. We tracked his horse right to where we found him."

"Well, that's good, if he was alone and you got the right man. If not, we got all we need for a ground war with God knows what nation."

"A ground war," said Jack. "Them days are long gone. Indians ain't gone on a warpath for more'n twenty years." Jack was looking a little smug.

"I ain't saying they might." Said Domingo." I'm saying it don't take much for a group of Indians to start attacking settlers' homes. You ever seen what a group of Indians can do to a family? Because I have. If this Indian hanging can be questioned at all, it will be. If you got the only one, then you are all I need to worry about. Vigilante hangin is against the law."

Domingo looked over to Axle again. "We need about six good men and supplies for a week or so. If there was more than one, or these fellas hanged the wrong Indian, we could be gone a while. Anyway, town's crawlin with Indians. We need to make a show like we mean to do well by them. We leave in the morning."

"Well you go ahead then," said Jack. He was feeling more than a little nervous. "Boss wants me back out at the ranch."

"Not so fast," said Domingo. "You're staying here. I'm going to need you in the morning. You're the only one here who knows where you left the hanged man. Even if you did get the right man, I'm going to need all the evidence I can get to prove it."

"Evidence," repeated Jack.

"Yes, evidence. I need to see the victim, and I

need a weapon, and I need them boots more than anything. What kind of gun was he carryin?"

Jack tried to remember if he had seen any gun.

"Ain't sure, he said. Must a been a rifle. He had no pistol I saw."

"So where is it?"

"Can't say," said Jack. "Thinkin on it, I guess I never saw that either, but he had to have one. He killed Brodie with it. Blew his heart right out of him."

"Get to it," Domingo told Axle.

Jack was locked up in one of the cells and Domingo set about readying rifles for the posse.

Axle had the six riders by suppertime, but couldn't get the supplies until morning. The trading post was closed. He could have rousted Owen Underhill but decided that morning was soon enough.

One of the riders Axle chose was a Nez Perce Indian named Tony Blackhawk. Tony had wandered down from northern Idaho, working ranches and about anything else he could find. He was not a drinking man. He rode an Appaloosa horse he had owned since he was a boy, and it was said of him that he could track a piss-ant through a corn field. Axle didn't think they would need a tracker, but if they did, he wanted the best he could get. Tony was it.

Morning found Janice Clanton up early. She was waiting at the trading post when Owen opened up. She gathered what she needed there, while Ed loaded feed sacks with Lacey. Axle Ford came in for supplies as she left the shop. Owen called his brother Bailey to come down and help. Axle loaded the counter with goods as fast as Owen could ring them up.

"This here is on the city," said Axle.

"The city?" Said Owen.

"Puttin together a posse. Looks like some Indian went and shot Brodie Buckhart."

"Do tell. Got any idea who?"

"Nope." Axle stopped short of telling of the hanging.

"What direction?"

"West, why?"

"Well, I was just about to ride out to look for an Indian, myself. Slicked me out of one my saddles yesterday."

"What are you saying?" asked Bailey. "That was a clean deal, as much as I could tell."

"Made a fool of me," said Owen. "I ain't wanting it back, but he owes me."

"You're nuts," said Bailey. "You can't find that kid. Even if you did, what you going to tell him? You agreed."

"I'm goin Bailey, that's all. You keep the store till I get back. Ain't no Indian getting the best of me like that. The whole town is laughing about it. Janice Clanton even brought it up this mornin. If all I do is save face, then that's all. Anyway, if I don't find him in a couple days I'll come back. At least I can say I made a show."

Bailey watched, a little dumbfounded, as Owen left the store behind Axle and headed for the stable.

The posse rode out of town at a lope. Owen was only about an hour behind them. Where Jack broke off the main road and headed for the hanging man, Owen held his course. He had not seen anything that would suggest that he was on the right trail but there were a few other tracks on the road and it was hard to tell. He found only one set of barefoot pony tracks that he decided might be anyone. His hope was that if Talon had gone west, sooner or later he would find some sign of him. If not, he would ride from town to town looking and asking questions.

It was around two in the afternoon when he got lucky. He had been making good time and had gotten all the way out to Twin Creeks crossing. At the crossing, he found two sets of barefoot horse tracks, a larger one and the somewhat smaller track of the packhorse. They were headed north. It was the best lead he had, and he figured it must be Talon. He remembered that the paint was a large horse, and Talon's pack was smaller.

He left the trail and pushed north. About dark, he found Talon's campsite. Talon was gone, but he only found one sleeping spot where a bedroll had been laid out and that could only mean one thing – the camp was made by one man with two horses.

The nights were well lit, and he thought about going on. He decided not to. The horses were barefoot and left a lesser track and he decided he might lose the trail in the dark, so he set camp and waited till day.

Chapter 12

Warm Night, Hot Trail

Domingo and his posse arrived at the hanging man in the afternoon. They had no problem finding the rifle but the boots and hat were gone.

"I'm tellin you, he had them on," Jack insisted. "There was one on him and the other was up there." He pointed up the hill. Domingo stood staring at him. He was sure that Jack was right, but he was feeling a little desperate for what he should do about the missing boots.

They had searched the hillside for fifty feet in all directions. The water had cleared enough by the time the posse arrived to see part of the 30-30, and they had that, but the boots were the thing they needed the most and they were gone.

Tony Blackhawk had walked the trail ahead of the hanging tree. He suddenly emerged from the heavy cover of the trees. The movement caught Domingo's eye. When He turned to see, Tony was looking at him.

"Well?" he asked.

"Your boots went that way," said Tony." They left on two barefoot horses, walking.

Domingo looked first to Axle and then to Jack.

"Not us," said Jack." We had all our horses shod. Someone else must have found the place."

Domingo looked around the place. It didn't look like the kind of place one might find easy. He looked back to Tony.

"What might we be looking for, Mr. Blackhawk?"

"White men use roads," said Tony. "They're easy targets. They also use horses with shoes. Most Indians can't pay."

"Alright," said Domingo, in a voice loud enough to be heard. "This is it. You there," he pointed to a stout looking man named Sam Edgewood. "You been deputized for the city of Wolf Creek. You go with Lambert back to the Buckhart place and try to get a look at the body. Take careful notes. I will need all the information you can squeeze out of him. Then you take this rifle," he handed him JR's 30-30," and take these keys to the office door and gun case. Until I get back you're the newly appointed sheriff of Wolf Creek. Guard that rifle with your life; it might depend on it. The rest of you mount up and stay close. Tony, you lead. You're the map reader."

The seven men and three packhorses left the hanging tree at a quick pace. The daylight was fading when they left the cottonwood, and they didn't get far before the moon was the only light there was. It was a mostly full moon and the light was bright where it could reach. They moved through the trees on the same game trail Talon took. Early in the night they came onto the east fork of Twin Creeks and followed it toward the road. Domingo rode directly behind Tony.

"How you doin? Tracks still visible?"

Tony turned in the saddle to look at him and then back to look forward again.

"Plenty tracks," he said.

He wasn't sure what Domingo meant. Full daylight would not have been any easier. Had Talon realized he might need to, he would have ridden up the middle of the stream. The water might have washed his tracks away in most places, but even that would not have fooled a good tracker for long. Tony could tell that Talon was not aware that he was being followed.

The night was cool and damp feeling. Stars sparkled brightly from the clear sky and the only sound that could be heard was the plodding of the horse's feet and the water in the stream. An owl hooted from somewhere to the west and a light breeze picked up as they came onto the road.

Owen Underhill was woken up in the night by the toe of someone's boot nudging him. He scrambled for his rifle in a panic. Domingo was holding it. When he discovered it gone, he sat up and scrambled back from his bedroll on his knees.

At first, all he saw was that his camp was full of people. He couldn't make out their faces in the moonlight, but his eyes did catch Domingo's badge reflecting light. He began to relax as the realization settled in that it was the law. What law he hadn't decided yet. There hadn't been any reason he had heard of for a federal marshal to be wandering around in the night but this was an unsettled land. Anything might have happened.

Domingo would have ridden past if Owen had not been camped in Talon's trail. He recognized Owen the minute he saw him. The night was getting deep, and he knew not to push the horses and men too hard.

Besides recognizing Owen, his camp seemed like as good as any place to bed down, and he decided to stop for the night. In any case, it would be interesting to see why the owner of the local trading post was camped out in the backcountry at all, much less in the trail he was following.

When Owen's eyes accustomed to the dark, he was able to see who was standing in front of him. "Domingo Wells," he said in a matter of fact tone. "Is that how you always wake folks up in the middle of the night?"

"Sorry," said Domingo, "fresh out of roosters. You on a fishing trip Mr. Underwood?"

Owen thought he could hear a little suspicion in Domingo's voice. He didn't like it. "No," said Owen, still a little put out at Domingo. "I just thought the ground might be a little softer than my nice warm bed at home. If it matters to you, I'm looking for an Indian."

"Well this might be your lucky night," said Domingo." I brought one with me."

"Well that was thoughtful of ya," said Owen, "but I doubt it's the right one. The one I'm looking for took me for a saddle. I aim to have a word with him bout that."

"What makes you think the one you're following is the right one?" Domingo wanted to know.

"It's my best guess. How many Indians you know that ride big barefoot saddle horses and need a pack animal. Seems this one plans on making trail for a while. So did the one I want. He bought a bit of grubstake at my place. The kind you need for a trip."

"Could be," said Domingo, "we're looking for the same man. We tracked him to your bedroll."

Domingo turned to the posse. "Make camp. I'll take first watch."

He turned back to Owen. "I had to send a man back to town. That left me one short. You better get some sleep. You just been deputized."

Owen wanted to argue. He wasn't sure he wanted to catch up to three feathers riding with a posse, but on the other hand, it might be better. He was no hand at cross-country travel. He also decided that he could easily lose the trail by himself. An escort might be nice.

He wondered why the sheriff had a posse after the kid. It had to be about the shooting of Brodie Buckhart, but the kid was still in town when Brodie got shot. Or was he? *Had to be,* thought Owen, *he came in with the Clantons. Oh well, sleep first then ask questions.*

CHAPTER 13

TRACKING THE TINY SPIDER

Talon maintained his trek north for most of the next day. He didn't know how far north he should go before heading more west again. He wanted to land in the Idaho territory far enough north to find the people with the spotted horses, the ones they called the Nez Perce, but still come in under the Blackfoot nation.

Times had changed and there was a new way of thinking now. Indians had, for the most part, stopped warring. That was good to know, but not enough to cause him to want to take any chances.

By afternoon, the lay of the land had started to push him farther west. The little ridges he had been using were hiding small dry valleys. The little valleys were easier to travel in than crossing from ridge to ridge on a more northern route. He judged by the sun and knew he was changing his direction more to the west again, but he was making good time. He decided that he could turn north later, and held to the little valleys.

The little canyon he was in wound back and forth and then opened into a large valley. He had just entered when the ears of the gelding shot forward. He was looking to the west and Talon saw why. There were antelope in the grass a half-mile ahead. He wished he had time to rig a snare of some kind and try to catch one in the night. The fresh meat would be nice, once it aged a little, but there wasn't time. He still kept a close eye behind himself.

The hanging man still haunted him a little. That feeling of trouble had stayed with him through the night. Besides that, there was Owen. Talon never caught his name but he had studied his face and kept thinking of what he saw there.

Owen seemed like a rather impatient man, but not a violent one. *Still,* thought Talon as he straightened his hat, *I have a lot to lose. Amazing new boots, nice hat, and the kind of clothes only the rich could afford.* Then he thought of the gift Janice said she had added to his clothes. He had forgotten that. He hoped it was food or cookies but didn't want to unpack to find out.

He had left the pack loaded, and manhandled it onto the horse this morning, for a fast escape from camp. *Should look at that,* he told himself as he rode on.

The valley was straight, and getting wider as he went and the day was fading. There were sagebrush and grass on most of the valley floor. It was scattered between aspen and juniper trees that left most of the bottomland open. An ancient dry wash meandered through the valley, and in places was too deep to cross. It would have been a good place to live any other time. He rode straight ahead for a while look-ing for a suitable place to camp.

Straight to his left, he saw a spot that looked greener than the rest. He had almost ridden past it before it became visible. It was over the top of a small hill he had ridden up onto. It was a small group of willows and aspen trees. There was a green carpet of grass for fifty feet around a rock outcrop-ping that jutted from the side of the valley wall.

He turned sharp to the left and rode the half-mile or so to the spot. It was a small spring, but only formed a puddle of usable water in the gravel and faded away. *Good place,* thought Talon. He dismount-ed and set about scooping out the spring to deepen it for the horses. He had a small cooking pot to dig with, and when the hole was about deep enough he hit bedrock. He watered the horses and filled his own canteen, then prepared his coffee for the morn-ing and set it aside.

After that, he decided to try the spring. It had hit bedrock. That could mean gold. The sand had a little quartz in it. It was rose quartz, the kind he had seen around where gold was found. The spot he was camped in was a good place. He could see his back trail for a good distance, and anyone following him might not notice it at all. They would head down valley and might miss seeing the spring.

It was getting dark, so he made camp. He lay and listened until he fell asleep.

The sun was up and getting warm before Talon rolled his bed and started the day. He ate a little and then decided to try the spring again. He thought about packing up and adding a few more miles between him and the hanging man, but the bad feeling was beginning to fade and if someone had been after him they should have shown up by now. It was midday before he gave up on getting rich and started out again.

The sun was getting hot, and sweat gathered under his hat brim. The wind had all but stopped. Talon followed the dry wash for a couple miles before he found a place to cross it. He slid down the side and had to ride along the bottom for a few yards before his horses could scramble back up the other side. He had traveled too far south by then and doubled back about three-quarters of a mile to get back on course.

The valley flattened out and turned to dust that clung to the sweat on his face. He was working his way to the north side of the valley when he climbed out of a little hollow he had been in. He had a good view of the lay of the land from here.

About ten miles ahead, the valley narrowed and turned south down what looked like it might be a rough canyon where the water had once flowed. He had seen places like it before. You could almost expect to come to spots where the water fell twelve or fifteen feet. It would leave him stranded and force a retreat back to where he was.

He needed a way out of the canyon. Going east would be in the opposite direction he was traveling. His problem was that north was almost straight up. He looked around for a better way, but in the end decided to try the north side of the canyon wall. It was steep but mostly buffalo grass and not much rock. There was a shale slide near the top, but it looked like he could avoid it. The side he was looking at was easily three miles high and steep.

His packhorse was packing less than two hundred pounds. *That would help,* Talon reasoned. The paint was strong enough that he sometimes wondered if the horse even cared that Talon was there. That was the good news. The bad news was that the hill in front of him was a long steep slippery climb. Stepping on dry buffalo grass was about like stepping on ice for anyone on a steep hill, but horses seemed to have little problem with it.

Most of the trip to the top was covered with it. If the ground turned out to be soft, as hilltops sometimes were, he could find himself sliding down in sandy soil and not be able to make the rest of the climb.

He looked around and would have liked to have found a better way up. After looking, he could see that the rest of the canyon wall was even worse.

Rock cliffs and shale slides made them impossible for man or beast.

It was around two in the afternoon when he began his climb out of the valley. He zig-zagged back and forth with a hundred feet or so in a pass, each pass a little higher than the last. It kept his horses from climbing too high in one burst and gave them better footing.

They climbed until near dark and were wore out and covered with sweat before they reached the top. As he did, he saw that he had ascended the hill to a nice point that overlooked the entire valley before him.

A large rim of rock the size of a storefront held the top in place. Beyond it, the land was open and somewhat flat. Talon stopped in front of the rock to rest his horses. From his resting place, he could see that he had been correct about the west end of the valley. It turned into a steep canyon, with sheer rock walls that reached up several hundred feet. The bottom of it fell away sharp and jagged. No horse, not even his, could have gone down it.

Back the way he had come, he could see the valley for fifty miles. The little draw he had followed into the valley was several miles behind him, and he could see the spring where he had camped the night before.

The horses were tired and Talon decided to dry camp for the night. He would need to find water for the horses in the morning, but they were better off resting.

A cool wind blew through the grass in little waves that rolled away with a soft peaceful sound. It was a peaceful place, and hard to notice from the bottom. After he hobbled the gelding, he left the horses cropping grass. A sandy spot up against the cool face of the rock served for a bed.

The trail had never looked so good. As far as he could see, the distant valley rolled out before him. For a dry valley, it was greener than one might expect. The little spring he had used was the only place he could see that looked wet.

Small islands of trees dotted the valley floor. In the distance, he could see occasional dust clouds tossed up by the wind. A red-tailed hawk drifted silently over the valley just below where he was setting. He always thought that they looked as if they were sleeping in the air when they did that. He had always wished he could fly like that, to just drift on the warm wind and rest there.

The steep bank of the valley was at his feet and he watched a flock of chukars fly by just below him. They landed in a brush clump not far down from his camp. The hawk had put them to flight by his presence. This was life at its best. Peace, and only the voice of the wind to hear.

The pack was within easy reach. It lay upright with the flap in place, and Talon remembered the gift Janice had told him of, when it caught his eye.

He reached over and dug around in the pack. There was a can of beans near the top. He opened them with his knife. Then he reached in again. The gift had been wrapped with his new clothes and he hated to unwrap them so soon. Dust would cake them if they got exposed on the trail. He lifted the bundle and carefully untied the cotton string that held the package together. The shirt was on top. It was soft and he couldn't resist pulling it out to look at it. The pants were extremely nice but he liked the shirt the best. The bright red and black stripes of fine wool was treasure to him. He folded it back the best he could and lifted the pants out next.

Janice had taken careful care of the way she had sewn the seam. It was perfectly straight. It was also double stitched. He inspected the belt loops and wanted to try them on again. They made him feel rich.

Then he remembered the gift again. He draped the pants over the pack saddle. In the bottom of the bundle was a small package. It was wrapped in the paper Janice used to cut patterns from. The paper was folded around whatever was inside. Talon unfolded the paper.

Inside was something made of the smoothest material he had ever felt. It was bright red and had a beautiful sheen that caught the sun and almost reflected it. When he unfolded the cloth it was an amazing bright red silk neck scarf. The scarf was the size of a small tablecloth, over two feet long. He had never heard of silk and had no idea what it was. What he did know was that this scarf looked very rich. It was so smooth that he could hardly feel it passing over the skin on his hand. Why anyone would ever give away such a thing he could not imagine. He would have worked five mean horses for something like this alone. Why she had asked him not to open it till he was on the trail he now understood. He could not have accepted it otherwise. On the Reservation, he knew men who would literally kill someone for a scarf like this one. He lifted it up and let the wind lift and toss it around. She had said that none of them would ever use it. *Strange* thought Talon, *she could easily have sold it.*

His eye caught something on the corner of the scarf. It had a design of some kind embroidered into it. Talon slid his hand down the smooth edge of the scarf to where it was, to inspect it. It was done in bright yellow thread that appeared to be made of the same smooth material the scarf had been made of. The design made no sense to him. It looked like a rainbow upside down with a small round circle inside of it. He inspected it closely and then ran the scarf over his hand again.

"What good fortune have I found," he said in a low audible voice. "Whatever god is following me. He is very good to me."

It brought him a feeling of suspicion. Things weren't just good, they were too good. When he had folded the scarf back up, he reached back into the pack. He found the boots and pulled them out. *Much too good,* he thought.

An idea came to him. He brushed a place on a large rock clean and unfolded the shirt. Then he laid it out on the rock. Next, the pants under it, like a man standing. After that, he put the boots in their place at the bottom. The scarf he put at the top of the shirt.

The wind tried to blow it away so he used small stones to hold it in place. Then he put the nice new hat on the very top. When he had finished, he stepped back to admire the set. He looked up and down it. He had become rich beyond his greatest dream.

I didn't go looking for any of these things, thought Talon. *They were waiting on the trail for me.* He hoped it wasn't a sign that he was about to die, or maybe that the cabin would be his end. He remembered that the story told of people who went in but never came out. Well, thought Talon, if I die then I die rich. And I die fearless.

He ran his hands over the fine clothes one more time, from the hat to the boots. He thought he should put the boots on. He had never really looked at them on his feet before. When he did, they fit like they had been made for him. When he stood up they were strong and snug feeling. They were the perfect addition to the clothes. In the end, he decided to save them as well. He would put on all of it some day at his cabin. He would do it, he decided, before he went in, just in case.

He took the boots off again and slipped his moccasins back on. It all seemed perfect. So why could he not shake the feeling that something was wrong? Like the price had not been paid in full. He looked around and his eyes fell on the new saddle. Not just a saddle, but a new one. It was the perfect size and made of the finest leather the army could buy. The head rig was as good. It sported a snaffle bit and was well designed. A horse would not be able to pull out of it even in a fight. The reins would break first. Was that it? Was the owner of the trading post coming for him? If so, he should be showing up any time now. It all seemed a little overwhelming. *The higher you climb*, he told himself, *the farther you must fall.* Or maybe he would have to learn to fly.

Whatever it was, he was going to need to be on alert now. Too much good might demand some sort of bad. He carefully folded the clothes again and wrapped the linen around them. The scarf he wasn't through looking at. When he was, he wrapped the paper around it and slipped it into the top of one of

the boots. They were securely tied inside the panniers. It would be safe there and he could reach it
easily when he wanted to look at it again. When he
had finished he ate his beans. Then he shook out his
bedroll and settled in. He found sleep easy.

Daylight comes earlier in high places, and Talon
was awake to watch it happen. He looked up the
canyon to the little draw he had entered from, and to
his surprise realized that there was a camp with
horses there.

They already had breakfast. Someone was
stomping out the cooking fire. As daylight began
to filter into the valley they packed their horses.
They looked to be in a hurry, to Talon. He watched
until the single-file string of horses began to line
out of camp.

There were about a dozen horses in all. Some of
them, Talon reasoned, would be packhorses. The
string rode the same path that Talon had taken.
When they got to the place he had first seen the
spring, they turned straight to the left, without

slowing down. Talon broke camp and waited to see what they would do next.

It was obvious that anyone who knew the country would not be in this end of the valley. They would know there was no way out. Besides that, why would there be so many men traveling together and why so far from any known road? They appeared to be following his tracks step for step. His rapidly pounding heart already knew the answer to his questions.

He waited until they had watered their horses and headed out again. They weren't wasting any time. They followed his tracks to the spot where he crossed the dry wash. Once in the wash, they chose the same route he had used even though it was not an easy one. An easier route might have been found with a little more effort, but they didn't bother looking.

They were coming for him. Did they think he was involved in the hanging of the Indian, or maybe that he was a part of what got the man hanged in the first place? He realized that he might have involved himself in about anything.

He had feared that the shop owner might follow him, but he would be alone. This looked like a posse, or it might be vigilantes. Vigilantes wouldn't be asking many questions. In any case, they were following his tracks from the hanging man. That alone would be enough to implicate him.

He was in trouble. He had lived like a hunted man very little in his life. Now and then, he had tried to stay out of sight, but he had never been the rabbit. Things had just gotten very serious. He reasoned that he had only two choices. Stand and face what looked like a fight against impossible odds, or run.

He calculated that he had about an eight-hour head start, counting the time it took to cross the valley. Their packhorses would no doubt be loaded heavier than his. That would slow them down. At the top of the hill, they also would need to rest the horses like he had.

He tried to remember anything he had heard, of

how to escape other men. The panic crept up his spine as he watched the riders move closer. There was one thing he had learned from working horses. Fear was a choice. Once he remembered that, he chose not to fear. The thought forced the panic out of his mind, and he began to reason.

Red Earth had talked of ways to cover a horse's tracks. He recited them in his mind. Stay in rock if you can. Move carefully; a stone bruise will leave your horse lame. You would need to leave him behind. High grass was another thing he remembered. If your trail wandered a lot in high grass it is harder to follow. His success would depend greatly on how good the tracker looking for him was. He had none of those things at the moment, but he had a good lead and a strong horse.

He headed north and braced for a long day. Night would not stop him to rest if he could see well enough.

There was no trail to follow on the top. Sagebrush four feet high carpeted the landscape before him. He was on a high bench that tapered off gradually. As far as he could see, the prairie beyond was flat little rocky tops with small draws between them. He tried to maintain a northwest direction, but the lay of the land made it difficult.

Hot dusty wind blew in his face and he worried if he would find water. Now and then, deer would bound away once they saw him, and one small elk herd watched him from a shallow ridge a half mile to the south. That told him there was water someplace not far away.

Anytime he found himself on a little top that was rocky he tried to walk on rock. On one of the little tops he started out north but while still on flat rock he switched back and headed south. The ridge petered out after a few hundred yards and he crossed to another one. Then headed north again.

By the end of the day, the brush was getting a lot shorter. Then it was gone and he found himself in rolling hills with little islands of pine trees and small dry clumps of grass.

Chapter 14

Intent to do Harm

Tony Blackhawk had been a lot of places since he left his reservation, most of them through back-country. There was a law that forbid Indians the right to leave the reservations, but it was an old law and not often enforced. Unless an Indian got into some kind of trouble or drew too much attention to himself, he was usually left alone.

Tony knew the law and opted to keep a low profile. To do that meant staying off main roads and trails when possible. Wandering was a risk, but it was a risk he was willing to take.

Most of the nations remained at home because it was home. The government aid they received there was needful and could not be obtained off grounds.

Among the nations were those who were young enough at heart to grow bored with reservation life, and began to wander. Tony Blackhawk was one of them. He had dropped out of Idaho territory about ten years ago and wandered all over the western states. He had always told himself he would go back home someday, but life is a busy place and he never had.

This valley he had tracked Talon into was one of the places he remembered. If Talon had taken the time to do a better search he might have discovered what Tony already knew. Tony led the posse to the place where Talon had left the valley floor. The group stood staring up the wall to its top in amazement.

"Well," said Domingo, "whoever he is he ain't afraid of much."

"You ain't plannin on climbing that I hope," said

Owen. "If it doesn't kill us it will turn our horses inside out. These pack animals will need a week off after a climb like that."

Domingo looked up and down the valley. He couldn't see another way out either. He looked up the steep wall to the top again and tried to track how Talon must have gone.

"Well, he made it," said Domingo. "We can't go back."

Owen had no intention of going back himself, he just knew that trying a fool's climb like the one in front of him was insane. He could see the steep canyon Talon had seen in the end of the valley. It was a no go. He was looking east when the movement of horses caused him to look back at the other riders. They were headed south toward the rocky canyon.

"Well that ain't any better," Owen called out from the tail of the string. "Sides it ain't in the right direction."

The party moved forward like they hadn't heard him. They were following Tony. Tony had said nothing when he turned to leave. He didn't need to. He knew where he was.

Where the valley turned to the south a mile or so ahead of Talon's trail, it hid an anomaly that was hard to see from the valley floor. It was inside the turn just behind a sort of ridge. The ridge made it invisible to anyone east of where it happened. It wasn't until you rode past the shallow ridge that you realized it was there. Tony had found it by following game trails from the top down.

Hidden by centuries of falling rock and tree-dotted brush, was a slashing draw up the side of the valley wall. It started about four hundred feet up from the bottom and ran all the way to the top. It was a shallow draw. About five feet deep and no more than fifty feet wide at its widest. Almost like a half-sunken road had been built on the side of the canyon wall.

The rock in the draw was water worn and looked like an old river bed. It appeared to be as old as the mountain itself. Like it had raised with the mountain from some prehistoric event. The slant of the little draw made it considerably longer than the route Talon had taken, but it was worth the ride. It was faster and easier on the horses.

The posse made the climb that took Talon almost seven hours in about two. Their horses were not nearly as worn down and rested up quickly on the top. Tony knew Talon was headed north and maybe west a little. He figured that a fast ride northeast would cut his trail and put the posse back on the tracks.

He led north a mile or so and then wanted to work more to the east.

The problem was the lay of the land. It was a rocky stretch of ground that had the little flat tops Talon had wandered into and tried to hide his trail in. Tony saw it as a problem. They would slow the posse down and could stone bruise one of the horses. He skirted it along its western edge hoping for a good chance to cross or get around it.

They had reached the valley rim about five miles farther west than the spot where Talon had. Skirting the rocky area pushed them even farther west and he was beginning to worry that he might have to double back to find the trail again if the bad area was very long. He was delightfully surprised to cut Talon's tracks where they left the rough country.

Without knowing it, Tony had taken a short cut. It was a stroke of luck he had not expected. They were close now and getting closer. They pulled up and rested the horses when they found the tracks.

"You sure these are his?" asked Domingo.

"They're his," Tony said.

He Bent down and broke off a grass stem. Using the stem he teased the edge of one of the tracks. It crumbled into the track as soon as he touched it. Then he used his doubled up fist to see if the ground in the bottom of the track had swollen from morning dew.

"Three, maybe four hours," he said.

Domingo was relieved. Even with the ground that Talon was covering, Domingo figured they would catch up to him that evening or the next day at the latest.

Tony wanted to stay there and rest the horses an hour or two. He knew that barring any surprises they would catch up the next day. Pushing the horses could backfire on them. If they wore them down, it would take a whole day to get them rested back up again. The day was getting hot, and the horses were tired, but Domingo wanted to keep moving.

"Tony might be right," said Owen." I could use a break myself. Anyway, we got a good jump on him don't we?"

Jeffery Baker was standing next to his horse. He had been recruited by Axle at Dandy's. He had other things to do, but a dollar a day is a dollar more than he had. Besides that, he had never hunted a man before and thought he might like it. He was a trail-hardened cowhand who drifted from town to town. He worked when he had to and spent his money on what he liked. What he liked was women, horses, and guns.

As well as riding trail, he had spent a lot of time riding the edge of the law. Nothing outright illegal, but if it paid well enough he would have. He was an impatient man, the kind who wanted a lot more than he was willing to put the time into getting.

Domingo had been watching him and decided that when it came to Jeffery Baker he had a lot more questions than answers.

"I ain't no law man," said Jeff, "but has it occurred to anyone that this here guy we're following ain't so innocent as we think?"

"I thought of that," said Domingo. "But Lambert said they followed the hanging man to the tree. He was alone."

"Ya, he was alone," said Jeff. "Unless he had a backup somewhere nearby. How did this fella find that hanging man anyway? Ain't like he was hanging in town square. I might not of found him if I'd a knowed where to look."

Domingo thought on what Jeff was saying. It did leave some questions. The horses they were following were barefoot animals. That meant the man with them was most likely the Indian Owen had done business with in town. He decided that Jeffery Baker might be right. He might need to bring this Indian back to Wolf Creek, at least until he could reason out what happened the night Brodie Buckhart died.

He looked around at his posse. They weren't much in the way of law enforcers. He wondered how long they would be able to stay on trail if the days dragged on. Owen he knew. He was a little overweight and not a good shot. In fact, it surprised Domingo that he even owned a gun. The only one he had with him was a handgun. Domingo doubted he could hit anything more than about ten feet away with it, unless it was one of the other riders, on accident.

The others amounted to Axle and five men whose faces he thought he had seen in town. He didn't know them at all, but you take what you can get in a place as small as Wolf Creek.

Four of the others seemed okay as far as he could tell. He hadn't had time to find out. This one, who called himself Jeffery Baker, seemed a bit of a loose cannon, and he spent most of his time riding next to one of the other men, whose name Domingo either forgot or never knew. They seemed to know each other from someplace else. Anytime there was a low murmur of voices behind him it was those two.

Two of the last three were men whose names he hadn't learned yet, but they looked okay. Just the average type you find anywhere. They were strong-looking and rode well. He hoped they could shoot if they needed to.

The last one was Tony Blackhawk. He showed up in Wolf Creek a while back and kept to himself. Domingo had seen him a few times and heard that he was a good sort, but didn't know him.

Axle did seem to know him. Axle knew about anyone who was around if they stayed around long enough. He had two days off a week and his off time he spent wandering around town asking questions, talking to people, and riding the prairie around the surrounding area. He was a man who noticed things.

Things like what shoes a man wore, and the cut of his clothes. If he was dusty a lot he most likely worked. Those types he wasn't too concerned about. It was the dusty ones that showed up in town new. They were usually fresh off the trail and deserved a little more attention.

If he was dressed well, he might be a gun hand looking for work. If not, he might be a gambler. That was something to keep up with. Sooner than later it usually meant trouble of some kind.

Gambling was a living for some people and Axle paid attention to who won a little too often and made note of it. On rare accessions, he had made a little spending money telling unsuspecting cowboys who not to gamble with. It saved a lot of bar trouble. Besides that, it kept him in good with the local ranch hands.

Domingo figured Tony for a good hand. Axle had hand picked him. He noticed that Tony was a loner. He rarely spoke and listened a lot. A man like that was a man who knew a lot more than he let on. When he did speak, people listened. Folks get to know a man more by what he don't say. If he does talk, they figure he has thought it through and knows what he is talking about. He was the tracker and rode lead. If Axle said he was trustworthy then that was good enough for Domingo. He didn't know if he liked all the men he had or not, but he needed help and might need witnesses.

The horses were a little lathered up and more rest would have been better, but they were losing time and he wanted this thing over with. It started out a tinder-box and might have just gotten even more so. If the Indian in front of them was involved, it might be a firefight when they caught up.

"What guns we got?" asked Domingo. "And how much ammo?"

Tony held up his 30-30. It was all he had. "Ten rounds," he said.

Owen had the six-shooter and six rounds. He pointed the pistol at his own face to check the ends of the bullets in the tumbler. Domingo shook his head. He was glad it wasn't cocked. Of the other three, there was a lever-action 44 rifle and a 45-70 with the two Domingo didn't know. Between them, they had 20 rounds. Five in each rifle and five in their saddle bags. Albert was carrying a 44 pistol. He had ten rounds also.

It was Jeffery Baker who raised Domingo's eyebrows. He was carrying a long gun. Domingo had never seen one like it. When Jeff pulled it from the scabbard on his horse the first thing Domingo saw was the scope mounted on the top. He had only seen a couple of them in magazines. He looked with suspicion at Jeff.

"Mauser 98," said Jeff. "Eight-millimeter, scoped for long shootin. This beauty was built in Germany, newest thing on the market. This rifle can hit a man 500 yards away every time."

"Why would anyone need a gun like that?" Axle wanted to know.

"No reason," said Jeff. "I like it. Three months wages for a piece of technology like this. Killed an antelope over four hundred yards away with it not long ago. You give me a rest, I can knock the pit out a peach at a hundred yards."

Jeff also had a 44 pistol. He was carrying six rounds in it. If Domingo ever had a reason to question trusting Jeff, it was that rifle. He began to wonder what kind of man would need one. It was too long for fast action and didn't seem like the kind of gun you might want in close. It didn't scabbard well on the horse either. Not like the normal saddle rifles he was used to seeing. He was a little surprised that he had not noticed it earlier.

"How many rounds you got?" asked Domingo.

"Five in the Mag, one more in the chamber," said Jeff. His hand slipped into the pocket of his coat to be sure. He had one more round there.

"I got six for the Mauser and six 44's, "he said.

Domingo wasn't sure if he liked Jeff or not, but he wasn't sure he wouldn't need him either. The horses had rested, and the party mounted up and fell back to the task at hand.

Domingo had to wonder why Owen Underhill had been on trail in the first place. He doubted it was the saddle. He knew Owen. Owen was a trader and a gambler. He was used to losing things.

All in all, he decided that if there was one to keep an eye on it was Jeffery. Then again, it might not be a bad idea to keep tabs on both of them.

CHAPTER 15

THINGS THAT GO BUMP IN THE NIGHT

Talon rode hard that day and into the night. The full moon was getting smaller and poor light in forested areas forced him to make camp sooner than he would have liked.

The terrain had changed again. The rolling hills had only lasted a few hours before they began to break into deep little canyons where there was usually water. Grass was plentiful and trees in the little bottoms grew thick.

The drawback was light. It got dark quicker in the bottoms. He camped that night in thick trees near a clear stream. The sound of the water was peaceful to him, and there was grass a plenty for the horses. He sat looking back down his trail with his back against one of the panniers.

The picture in his mind of the posse behind him was haunting. He figured they were no more than ten hours behind him and maybe a little less. They would have no problem keeping his trail if they found it where he left the rough place. That bothered him. In their shoes, he knew he would not have been fooled long.

The little green valleys were a welcome reprieve from the dry tops and sun backed hillsides but he knew they would not always take him in the best direction. Besides the water, their best advantage would be that his tracks would be harder to find. He couldn't run as long into the night but neither could they. They would know that he could leave any one of the little valleys up one of the draws that fed down to them anytime. In the dark, they would lose him.

Daylight found both parties on the trail. Tony knew that he and the posse were only a few hours behind Talon and pushed hard to catch up. Talon only knew that he was being followed by a large party of men, who he didn't expect would give up easy.

His plan was to hold north and west as always. He wanted to stay in the well-watered little canyons as long as he could. It worried him what they might do if they caught him. He was making good time along the small streams and decided that ten days at his present speed should be enough to shake them.

For nine days the posse worked hard to find Talon in the little canyons. He had crossed where he needed to in order to keep his direction, but for the most part, he had ridden hard down long stretches of brushy bottomland.

Tony had begun to realize that Talon somehow knew he was behind him and wanted for another shortcut. He knew that as long as Talon stayed in the little canyons there would be none.

A man on a horse could make a lot better time in

the bottoms than crossing all the little draws that fed them by trying to work the rims.

Anyplace where Talon had noticed a good draw coming down into the canyon he was in, he used it, especially if he needed to cross the little stream to get close to the mouth of the little draw. He would skirt the mouth of the draw but maintain his direction. Tony got the message. Talon was saying *I can leave the canyon any time, and if you're not in my tracks you will have to double back to find my trail.* It was the message that told Tony Talon knew he was there.

On the evening of the ninth day, Talon decided to check his success. He was running out of supplies and wanted time to hunt and cook meat. That would take a full day and he wanted to be sure he had a full day to spare. He hoped whoever was after him had given up. His plan was to wait the ten hours he expected they were behind him and find out.

He left his horses and camp in the grassy bottom and climbed up the first draw that led out of the bottom on foot. When he reached the top he stopped to watch the trail he had ridden down that day behind him. It would soon be dark.

He planned to stay on the rim for that night and at least most of the next day. The bottom that lay before him was long enough that he would have at least a two-hour jump on anyone he saw in his back trail.

A campfire would show up like a lantern in the dark down there and he would see it. His idea was good, his timing, not so much.

Just after dark, a campfire flared about where he expected it would. It was where a canyon had worked out of a lot of tight turns and narrow trails. It was the first place wide enough to camp in for a good long way before it.

He watched the fire burn in the distance. It was too far away to see anything more than the fact that it was there. *It couldn't be them,* thought Talon. They could not have gained on him that fast. He tried to think if he had seen any sign of humans in the bottoms. During the last ten days, he had seen a lot of elk and deer sign but no horses or humans. That would have been what he expected.

He was miles from any kind of settlements or towns. The last human sign he had seen was the posse. That of itself was not proof of anything, but the idea that someone was behind him and hot on his trail seemed strange to him. For a moment he was undecided as to what he should do. They were too close for comfort.

He had planned to have a two-hour jump on anyone showing up the next day. That wasn't much, but if he covered his tracks well enough he could slow them down. Then if he moved fast and got out of the canyon to the tops he would be able to gain ground while they unraveled his trail.

He really didn't think anyone would stay on his trail this long. They would be as low on supplies as he was. If they were that desperate to catch him, he was more important than he first thought. He figured it must not be the same party that had camped in the bottom behind him.

Still, thought Talon, *it would be stupid to take that chance.* He thought of breaking camp and riding through the dark of night, but what if it wasn't them? He needed to know.

As he watched the fire he began to hatch a plan. He would need to visit the camp in the dark. Even in poor moonlight, he should be able to see what he needed to know. The chance that it could be the same men was small, but if it was, he needed a way to slow them down or stop them if he could.

That was where his plan came in. He returned to his camp and pulled an old leather backpack from the panniers. It had been a gift from someone on the reservation. It was in the stuff Red Earth had in the pile from his neighbors. If he discovered by some off-chance that it was the same men he might be able to solve two problems with one trip. He hobbled the paint and put the saddle on the pack mare. She had been packing less and would be fresher. He might need the paint in fresh condition.

It took a little more than an hour to make the trip

down the ridge. The light was poor and he couldn't afford to be heard if he dislodged a rock. When he was still far enough away to be safe, he tied the mare and continued on foot.

Where the camp was, he slipped over the edge of the rim. As silently as the night, he descended down the wall to a point about a hundred feet above it. From where he now stood he could see the whole camp below him.

First watch was still on. The guard was sitting near a small fire. He was leaning back on a saddle that was on the ground behind him. It looked to Talon like he was not all that awake.

Horses, if they get loose, and decide to leave a camp will do it the same way every time. They always go back the way they came. Never forward. For that reason, Tony had kept the horses between the posse camp and Talon's. That way if they got loose they would have to go through camp and past the guard to escape. It was a good idea and would have worked if the horses had no one to interfere.

Talon studied the camp for a good while. He couldn't see anyone's face but he could easily see how many they were. There were seven bedrolls. Counting the guard made eight. They had four packhorses and all of them were in a spot just a little out of the light of the dying fire. There was little doubt that he was looking at the same men he had seen in the big valley he climbed out of ten days ago.

The guard was watching down the canyon the way they had come and Talon was not able to see his face. He wondered if it was Owen Underhill, still mad about the saddle trick. The guard's head was dropping a little and then jerking up again.

It didn't look like they were expecting company. It was amazing that they had gotten so close so fast. Talon tried to reason how they could have. They were a bigger party than he was and should have been slower. He decided that they must have been riding the ridges and hoping to not miss him, but how could they know where he changed from one canyon to the next? He supposed that it was possible that they were just heading north and hoping they could catch him by surprise. *That would be foolish*, thought Talon. Still, here they were.

He silently slipped down the canyon wall and into the camp. Staying along the edge he crawled up to where the horses were tethered. When he had carefully untied them he led them slowly back the way he had come until he reached the place where he had dropped into the bottom.

At that point, he started them out at a trot and let them go. The half-asleep guard didn't realize what was happening until the last horse was trotting past. Without a sound, he lunged out for the lead rope dragging behind the last horse. His rifle was left on the ground as he went. He missed the rope but was close to it and kept after the horse. A few seconds later, he disappeared into the dark brush beyond camp.

Talon waited for a moment to be sure nobody had awakened. Then, as silently as he could, he began to unload as much of their supplies as he could carry in his pack from their panniers. He filled his pack and then quickly worked his way to the edge of the little stream where the ground was loose and buried the supplies. When he was finished he did it again.

He was watching for the guard all the time but he never showed. When he finished the second trip he filled his pack and set it at the edge of camp. He had made off with most of their grubstake. *That should slow them down,* thought Talon. *They'll have no choice but to hunt. While I make tracks.*

The sleeping camp remained sleeping. When he felt safe enough, he put the pack on and climbed the canyon up to the point of his first roost. He watched for the guard to return from there but saw no sign of him.

He figured it was around two or so in the morning. The guard had been gone around twenty minutes. Moving as silently as he could, he returned to the camp.

He went first to the little fire of the guard. The

rifle was lying where it had fallen. It was not like anything Talon had ever seen. He held it to his shoulder and tried to see through the scope, but all he could see was dark. *Not good for night,* thought Talon. He knew what a scope was. He had seen pictures of them in ads to sell rifles at the reservation trading post. He had never held one.

The rifle was new to him also. It looked almost new and was made different than any he had seen. He thought of taking it. He looked it over again and then pulled the bolt open slowly. A cartridge popped out and hit the ground. In the rifle were more. He could see them in the top of the magazine.

Using the bolt to get them seemed like it would be a lot of noise. He decided to use his knife and ejected them manually. When he finished he put the rifle down where it had been. It would be too long to carry, and he didn't want the extra weight on the pack.

One at a time, he visited all the bed rolls in camp. As much as anything, he wanted faces. He found them. There was only one he recognized. It was Owen Underhill, the owner of the trading post.

Six white men and one Indian, but no one he knew. Before he left camp, he made one more silent trip through the sleeping camp. He stopped at a bedroll at the end of camp. Near that bedroll was Domingo's 45-70 rifle. He thought about taking it as well but decided he wouldn't need to. He figured they had reason enough to follow him as it was. Then he slipped out of camp and disappeared into the night.

Chapter 16

Running the Risk

It was getting daylight when the guard returned with the horses. The canyon was narrow and the horses had kept a good trot in single file down the only trail leading out. The guard had caught the last horse in the string after about ten minutes of trying. He threw a half hitch over its nose and rode it bareback.

He caught up with the other horses not long after, but couldn't get around them to the lead horse. It forced him to wait until he came to a place where the canyon widened enough to get past the string to the lead horse.

He arrived as the camp began to awaken. Domingo realized as daylight hit his face that he had overslept his turn at guard and came awake with a start. His rifle was leaning against a rock ten feet away. Not where he had left it. He lunged for it and lifted it to a hip shot position. In an instant, his eyes scanned the camp. Tony had his pistol in one hand. The gun belt was in the other. He had awakened a little before Domingo.

The sound of horses caught his attention. He whirled in the direction of the pounding hoofs. He was still a little fuzzy-headed but not so much so that he couldn't tell what he was looking at.

It was Jeffery Baker, the guard that he was to relieve four hours ago. Something was not right. He was riding bareback and leading the horses.

His eyes went from the horses to the rest of the camp. He noticed that the packs had been sacked. There was still stuff laying about where Talon had left it. It didn't take long to put things together.

"Roll out, yelled Domingo. "We got trouble."

Jeff Baker slid off the horse and picked up his rifle. It was leaning against the saddle. He had forgotten it until he was almost back to camp. It looked okay, but he knew he had not left it there with the bolt still open.

"Someone check those supplies," continued Domingo. It unnerved him that someone had stood over his body while he slept. It could only be one person. He walked to the burned-out cooking fire, scanning every inch of the camp as he went. On a small flat rock next to the fire ring, was one 45-70 round of ammunition. It was standing straight up like a little monument. Tony was staring at it. When Domingo saw it he stopped in his tracks. In an instant, he realized what had happened.

"Check your weapons," he called out. The sound of rifle bolts opening sounded off the canyon walls. "Empty," said Albert.

"Mine too." It was Allen Roth.

The men all checked their weapons. Not a one had any ammunition. Allen had saddle bags and they had been emptied out onto the ground.

"He went through everything," said Albert.

"Who was guard?" yelled Allen Roth.

He was one of the other two riders. He had bedded down not far from Walt Bates. They were standing a short way from the fire ring.

"I was," said Jeff, "the horses broke and I went after em."

"Just like that?" asked Owen. "You just left the camp unguarded without a word?"

"What was I supposed to do? The horses were headed out of camp at a fast trot. I like to not caught em as it was."

"Never mind that," said Domingo. "We can deal with that later."

"Never mind nothin," said Albert. "We could all be dead right now. He was watchin us sleep. Could have sent us to hell one by one, while our guard here left without a sound. You was sleepin wasn't ya?"

Jeff was red from his forehead to his shirt collar. "I was just standing there and they went by. Awake not sleepin."

"You're not dead because he didn't want you dead," Interrupted Tony.

The talk stopped and all eyes fell to Tony.

"He stopped by to get supplies and slow us down."

"Tony's right," said Owen. "Killin takes a lot of work and someone might call out. This way he just made a rough trip a lot rougher."

"Now that you bring that up," said Jeff, "what about Tony? This guy wanders around camp like he belongs here and no one wakes up. Not even our tracker and trail guard. He's an Indian himself. Maybe they were together on this one."

"He got his ammo too," said Domingo, "so I doubt that. If I was to ask who might have helped him pull it off I would be more apt to be lookin at you."

"That's insane," protested Jeffery, "I told ya I was after the horses."

"I ain't sayin you did, I'm sayin that's where I would look if I was lookin. I ain't lookin. It is what it is. We got no ammunition and we got a lot less sup-plies. Allen you been cookin. You check what's left of our supplies. I need to know how long we can go on what's left. The rest of you start breakin camp."

"Break camp," said Albert. "You ain't plannin on goin on after him I hope. We got no ammunition. He has plenty of it. Anytime he wants to he can pick us off like bottles on a fence rail."

"Yes I am still goin after him," said Domingo. "He has evidence of a murder and a hangin. Besides that, he might know a lot more than I used to think he did. Right now he's a criminal on the run."

"A well-armed criminal," said Albert. "That's suicide. I don't care what the law says. I ain't goin!"

Domingo looked over at Allen.

"Not much left," he said, "If we move out on what supplies we got now we won't make it three, maybe four days."

Domingo looked around camp. He figured Tony was right. They were alive because Talon wanted them alive. What he didn't know was why. That was a very pressing question. As he saw things, he was sitting on a hot load that could go off anytime. He needed the man on the barefoot horses, dead or alive. Stopping was out of the question.

The supplies were too short for a group this size and they had very little ammunition. It came to him why Talon had left the one cartridge behind. He intended that the posse would have to use it to hunt enough meat to get back to Wolf Creek. Even if they chose not to go back, it would buy him time. A hunt would take at least one day. It wasn't a move a criminal mind would think of. Anyone else would have left them with nothing. It looked to him like a statement. At the moment the man they were following had all the cards and the deck was stacked against the posse. Without ammunition, and running so low on other supplies they would be foolish to go on. Talon, on the other hand, was well supplied and would be well ahead before they got what they needed to follow. All the more reason to give up.

Where Domingo stood he wished he "could"

give up. The whole posse stood looking at him. It was his call. Running out on a posse was against the law and cowardly, so they waited. Being sent away was another thing.

"We can't all go anyway," said Domingo. "It's the last thing he will expect us to do and I'm goin. If he thinks we are without ammunition maybe he won't shoot until I can get close enough to get some answers. Meanwhile, I'm sending some of you back.

"Axle, you're the man I trust most of all these I got with me. For that reason, I need you to get back to Wolf Creek and cover for me. We been gone way too long. It's been eatin at me for days. All we got at home is one inexperienced deputy who won't know what to do, and might do more harm than good."

Axle wasn't impressed with Domingo's idea but he knew he was right. He felt like he was leaving Domingo in a bad spot. Trusting men like Jeffery Baker to cover your bet could get a guy killed, but orders were orders.

"Of the rest of you," said Domingo, I'm sending

back Albert," he looked around, "Allen, Walter and you," he pointed to Owen.

A sudden panic shot across Owen's face. "I ain't goin back, he said, I didn't start this ride to go back on account of things gettin a little rough. Send him back, he pointed to Jeffery, he's the one who caused this mess."

Jeffery started to protest but was interrupted by Domingo. "Much as I hate to think it, I might need him. He has the most ammunition in camp." He looked over to Jeffery. "You were wearing that gun belt when you cut out last night weren't ya?" asked Domingo.

Jeffery nodded his head. "I also got this," he said. He pulled the one eight-millimeter round out of his pocket. He held it up and then loaded it into the Mauser.

"How many 44 rounds you got?" asked Domingo.

"Jeffery pulled the pistol from its holster and looked down at it. "Six, just need one load most of the time. Just for protection."

"You got the rifle," said Domingo, I'm taking your 44 ammo."

"You got your 45-70," said Jeffery. "It has the same number of rounds I got."

"Hand em over or go back with the others and I will keep Allen."

Domingo wasn't sure which might be better, and didn't care. Jeffery on the other hand did. He had made up his mind to kill his first man on this hunt. He was thinking of it all along, but after what had been done to his reputation by Talon he was sure of it. One less Indian in the world seemed like a good thing to him anyway.

Jeff begrudgingly unloaded the pistol and handed the six rounds to Domingo. He looked over at Owen as he handed over the 44's. He didn't like Owen much, and giving up his ammunition didn't set well with him either. His problem with Owen was the constant complaining. He was sore, or the ground was hard to sleep on, or it was too hot, you name it. Owen was just not a trail hand.

"The only good thing about this," he said, "will be gettin rid of you. At least it will be a quiet suicide mission."

"Well I wouldn't get settled into that notion just yet," said Owen. "I ain't leavin. I would have gone back from where you fellas picked me up. Turns out I ain't much of a trail hand. Catching up with Three Feathers would take someone with more trail knowin than I got. After the sheriff here deputized me, I couldn't have quit if I wanted to. Anyway, it worked for me, for the better. I needed the use of a good tracker and you boys have one.

"Besides that, it's bad enough the whole town knows an Indian kid outsmarted Owen Underhill. Had a woman in the shop the very next morning snickerin about it with my brother Bailey. If you think I'm goin crawlin back into town with my tail between my legs now, I ain't. They'd say I ran out when the goin got rough. I got my honor to think about."

"You say his name is Three Feathers?" asked Domingo.

"Who knows, don't remember him ever sayin. I call him that..." Owen paused, "on account of he has three feathers in his hair."

Jeff wondered what Owen meant by Talon out-smarting him, but it was only a passing thought.

"We don't need him," protested Jeffery. "We ain't got enough food as it is."

Domingo looked back over at Owen. He hated to admit it, but Jeff was right. He was about to say so but didn't get the chance before Owen interrupted his thought.

"Anyway," he said, "I ain't goin back. I know there's a law about cuttin out on a posse, but I never heard of one that stops a man from goin on after he's been asked to leave. I can feed myself if need be. I ain't plumb dumb. I saved some of my own grub. If you let me stay I will add it to the rest."

"So why didn't you add it before?" asked Jeff.

"It wasn't needed before, and a man can't never count on tomorrow."

Domingo looked at the men standing around. They were waiting for him. He really didn't need Owen, but he did need at least four men. The only thing he had going for him without ammunition was numbers.

If he was going to keep another man he would rather have kept Allen Roth. Allen was the solid, no bluff type. Smart enough to know when he should fight, and fearless enough to do it if he needed to, but Owen had supplies, and even if he only had a few supplies, they were needed. He thought about just commandeering them and adding them to the cache for Axle to get back on, but Owen already said he would go on his own.

Anyway, Owen was getting a lot more saddle-hardened and trail able. He wasn't complaining like he had been, and if it was only for the numbers he was one more man in the saddle. He looked down at the six rounds of ammunition he had in his hand, and then back to the men. "Ok," he said, "we got six pistol rounds, one round in the Mauser and one in my rifle."

Domingo stepped over to his bedroll and picked up his 44. He loaded the six rounds into the tumbler and handed the pistol and belt to Axle.

"Axle, you take Allen, Walter, and Albert. High tail it back to Wolf Creek and hold down the fort until I get there. All you men will remain deputized until my return. Axle will be acting sheriff. You answer to him. The rest of you will stay with me."

Jeff glared over at Owen, who smiled back.

Domingo left camp that morning with four riders and two packhorses. He had enough supplies to last only about four days, but it was enough to keep moving and hope they were able to catch Talon. He really wasn't sure that Talon wasn't somehow involved in the shooting but he doubted it. No killer would have gone through a camp of sleeping men and not just quietly killed them.

At the very least he would have destroyed all the supplies he couldn't carry. This man had left just about enough supplies to get them back home. He also had left the horses unharmed. He could have stolen them out of camp and hamstrung them. The Apache wouldn't have thought twice about it.

He wondered if he shouldn't be more concerned about Jeff than the one they had come to call Three Feathers. Jeff was a threat, the kind of man who could be a danger to his mission. If he got a shot at the fugitive, Domingo was sure he would take it. He was also sure he wouldn't ask permission first. If he did, all the evidence and knowledge that Three Feathers had might be lost. The bad part was, it would fly in court. If Three Feathers did have those boots it's all any lawman would need to justify shooting him to stop him. Domingo would have little he could do to Jeff for the shooting.

Jeff only had one round for the rifle, but Domingo was a pretty good judge of character and figured that was all he would need. On the other hand, if Three Feathers started shooting, Jeff might be their best hope of surviving.

Tony took the lead position as usual. He studied the canyon walls to be sure they weren't riding into a trap. It bothered him that Talon had managed to steal his ammunition while he slept. In fact, it threatened him. He had let down his guard. Talon should have been farther ahead than that. He must have waited for them to catch up. Tony hadn't counted on that and wasn't keeping his edge well.

He reasoned that if Talon was that fearless, he might decide he was tired of running and start fighting. After all, as far as he knew he had all of their ammunition. What's more, he could easily ambush them from the top of the canyon at any moment.

That one round that Talon had left behind, the one he obviously meant them to kill game with, was his only comfort, and very little comfort it was. Did Talon only mean hunt and use the meat to get back, or was he saying "Here's your last chance? Go while you can. Next time we meet, death will find you before you hear the gun go off."

Domingo wasn't feeling any better than Tony

about the situation. He knew he was following an Indian, and he hoped he was right about him not being the violent type. There would be questions, but that was all he expected to need. Riding in the narrow canyon made him feel vulnerable, an easy target for a man who wanted one.

There was another thing that he found concerning. Owen rode tail. He always rode tail, even when he had to put up with a lot of dust from the other horses. He had developed the habit of drifting back until he had a good distance between him and the next horse. Domingo had begun to wonder why. If Owen was thinking that he had a safer place there he was wrong. At least he was wrong if this Indian fought like the Apache fought. He would be the first to die.

Then there was the possibility that he knew more than he was willing to say. He was the only one in the group who had ever laid eyes on the Indian. Did he know this Indian better than he was letting on, or was he just a good gambler? Axle said Owen was a good man to steer clear of in a poker match. Maybe he just had the man pegged and trusted his intuition. In either case, it was odd.

He thought of joining him at the end of the line to try to find out his thinking. He thought better of it. The last thing he wanted was to arouse any suspicion. It wouldn't do to make it appear as if there were secrets being kept from the others.

Owen was thinking some things through himself. He kept remembering Talon's face. Outside of the fact that he had one of the best poker faces Owen could remember, he seemed easy going, even to the point of maybe being a little shy. That was why his poker face had fooled him. He might have realized the trick otherwise. *Might not have been a good poker face after all,* thought Owen. *He had used the situation to his advantage, kept me off guard until he sprung the trap.*

He hoped he was right. With enough pressure, Three Feathers might decide to try to take the last man out, and if he didn't kill him, he would get his business out of the way early on. If on the other hand, Jeff killed the kid first, he might not get his business out of the way at all.

He needed a way to declaw Jeff. He thought of trying to steal that last cartridge in his fancy rifle. That would be difficult at best, now that their camp had been raided. He would be sleeping light. He thought on it all day. It was a problem. Jeff was another reason he liked the tail position. Owen was a good judge of people. There was a part of Jeff he didn't trust. Something in his face, or maybe it was his body language.

A gambling man would say Jeff had some sort of trick up his sleeve. Owen figured the trick was the Mauser and an itchy finger, a very itchy finger. Jeff did have an itchy finger, and now that things were what they were, it was a lot itchier. He held the 8mm in his arms and hoped he would see his target before he was seen by him. He had been played for a fool. Now it was personal.

CHAPTER 17

THAT WHICH WAS NOT

Talon started the day as soon as he got back to camp. It was still mostly dark, but the horses he had were mustangs. They would be okay till daylight.

He needed to get as much distance as possible between him and the posse. The work he had done in their camp had been risky. If he hadn't been desperate he would not have tried it. He hoped it had worked. They would not be wise to follow now. The only ammunition he thought they had was the one round he left in camp.

He couldn't remember if the guard had been carrying a pistol or not. Even if he had, it would not be enough ammunition to risk a gunfight with. Besides that, he wasn't their only threat. There were other Indians that might not take well to a lawman wandering around in backcountry either.

If they did still want him, then it might come to a fight. He would need to decide that later. He had never thought of killing a man before. It sounded easy when the elders talked of it. They spoke of the days of old when life required the death of something all the time. Their words were stories of some lost times to him, times he would never see. He wondered how it would have been in those days, to ride in the war parties against the Crow and Snake, but that was all past now.

The days of the Indian wars had passed before he was old enough to remember them. He was glad for that. He would have killed in those wars, he knew, but now things were not like that. Peace had become more important.

The Lakota had discovered that fighting with the white man was futile. They had lost too many good braves, and even whole villages in those days. Now all the buffalo were gone anyway. There was little left to fight over. It had brought about another day. He had been raised in a world where Indians were not even allowed to fight each other. In a way that was good. In another way, it left the young men with no way to prove themselves. If it came to a fight for his life, he decided that he could kill. He hoped it wouldn't come to that.

He had enough supplies to last a couple weeks at the very least, and at the moment there was plenty of water and grass for the horses. The sun rose warm and bright and the air stood still. Songbirds began flitting from tree to tree as soon as the light filled the little canyon he was in.

The paint's ears perked forward and he stopped to look at something in the brush not far ahead. It turned out to be a coyote. The coyote hadn't noticed them yet and was sniffing the ground as he wandered over it through the trees and rocks.

Talon hadn't seen any sign of game for a while. The gelding moved on after he had watched the coyote for a while. A few seconds later, the coyote noticed him but didn't seem too alarmed. *Must not be used to humans on horses,* thought Talon. If Talon had been on the ground it would have spooked sooner.

A little later, a cottontail crossed the trail and hid under a large rock. The trail began to wind now through more large rock and Ponderosa Pine. The grass was getting less all along, and the floor was more rock and sand. Talon looked up to check the walls of the little canyon. He wished he could find a way out if he needed one. At the moment there was none.

A rim of rock ten feet high lined the top of the canyon rim on both sides. The canyon was still wide enough to offer hope of opening up into a larger, safer place to be. He suddenly realized that he was following the little stream downstream. That was something he had noticed but hadn't really thought about. It could mean trouble. Most of the time it would mean the bottom of the canyon would flatten, then widen and in time join a larger drainage in some larger valley but not all the time.

He kept watch on the tops all day long. In a few places the rim broke off and he could have climbed out if he had really needed to, but one by one he passed them up for the canyon floor where he could make better time. It was also easier on the horses. Anytime he could, he rode up the side of the canyon to try to get a look at his back trail.

The trees were too thick most of the time and all he could see was a winding canyon behind him. When he got high enough he stopped and waited to see what the paint could see. The wind blew back down the trail he had come down so no scent of any other horses would be on the wind. That was not a good thing.

He listened for any sound that might give away activity behind him. The distance between him and the posse could not be much more than two or

three hours. He realized that he had lost time between their camp and his. Still, he hoped that he
might get a look at any followers if he could find a
place where the canyon was straight enough and
he was high enough.

By evening he had not had any luck. Heavy
clouds had moved in. The promise of a dark night
lay ahead and the rocks had gotten larger and more
numerous. At the last light, he was forced to camp
almost at the edge of the creek. That was the last
place he wanted to be. Predators worked the stream
sides at night. The water rushing by was another
reason he disliked being too close to the stream. He
couldn't hear anything.

Where he camped, the canyon had narrowed to
less than five hundred feet wide and was mostly
rock and sand. It wasn't looking good. Places like
this had come and gone in the past and had not been
a problem. This one might also. If not, he might need
to climb out. Looking up with the last light of day, he
studied the canyon for a break in the rock that would

let him escape the canyon. As the night settled in he had not found one.

The cool night air drifted up the canyon and Talon made a cold camp behind a large rock outcropping where the ground was loose. He lay still and tried to hear anything he could. As he passed into sleep all he could hear was his own horses and the water.

Dark fell fast in the canyon where Tony made camp. He had been in Talon's tracks all day. They were not hard to follow. As he looked down the canyon in the direction they led, he wondered if Talon knew he was still behind him. It didn't look like he did. The tracks had been too easy to follow. They had stayed in the trail and not slowed down. As far as he could see, Talon had not stepped out of his saddle all day. Neither had Tony. He knew he was close to Talon but not as close as he wished he was. Talon was tough to catch up to. He had given them a long hard ride and if it had been up to him he might have quit, but the money was okay and he was headed in a direction he liked. It was the trail home.

Talon was not in the same canyon Tony had traveled years ago when he left his people, but he was headed in the right direction and in the same country. Wolf Creek was becoming a memory now. He was not so far from his own people. Thoughts of the life he had left so far behind were starting to wander in like they had been resting on the breeze, resting and waiting where he had left them.

The sound of the land at night was different in the tall pines and fir trees. The nighthawk and meadow frogs were not as common on the drier prairie land. He had almost forgotten the smell of the trees and wild roses of home. Now he could feel more than he could see.

As the dark clouds gathered overhead, he looked

for a place to sleep where he could stay out of the rain if it started. The air was damp and cool. He had been watching his horse all day for any sign that Talon's horses might be close enough to smell. Once in a while, his ears had perked forward but it had been some other thing that caused it.

Often, if one horse smells another one he will give some sign of it – a snort or whinny or even just a quicker step to catch up. Sitting by the night fire, he wondered how far away Talon was. His horse had not offered any clues.

After they ate, Jeff put his saddle on the ground next to the fire and leaned back against it. The Mauser was leaning against a rock a few feet away. Domingo was at the outskirts of camp. He had first watch.

Owen rifled through his pack and found a deck

of cards. He sat down a couple feet from Jeff and shuffled them as loudly as he could. In the process, he dropped a couple of them on the ground and then put them back into the deck again. He had put them in face up, opposite the others. Jeff watched him attempt to shuffle the cards. Again and again, he lost a couple on the ground.

After a couple tries he had the cards shuffled and sorted so that they all faced the same way. Jeff watched silently while Owen fumbled around and got the cards like he wanted them.

"Life's getting a little boring round here," said Owen. "You up for some poker?"

Jeff was tired, but he thought he saw an opportunity.

"What's your ante?" Jeff asked.

Owen gave him a blank look.

"What you bettin with?" Asked Jeff.

"Oh," said Owen, "money. You know what that is, right?"

Jeff already didn't like Owen. He took that for an

insult. "How much you got?" he asked. He had a sneer on his face.

"Well don't get all huffy," said Owen, "Just makin a little fun."

Jeff wasn't amused.

"I got one dollar," said Owen, "how bout you?"

Jeff fished around in his pocket and found a silver dollar. He dropped it on the ground in front of Owen.

"Good," said Owen. He started to deal the cards.

"Where is it?" Jeff asked.

"What?"

"Your dollar." He was getting a little irritated.

"Oh that," Owen said, "I got it." He laid the cards down face up and started fishing around in his pocket. Jeff shook his head. *Fool, this ought to be easy,* he told himself.

Owen put a paper dollar on the ground and picked up the cards again. After he blew the dust off them he dealt out two hands on the ground. Jeff picked his hand up.

"You only gave me four cards," Jeff said. "If this

is poker, you're supposed to deal five."

"You got five," said Owen. "Can't you count? I'm lookin right at em."

"You ain't lookin at nothing," barked Jeff." I got four." He held the cards two in each hand to prove his point.

"You're a fool," Owen snapped back. "You got five. You're just trying to get more."

"I ought to break your fool nose for that!" Jeff roared. He really did want to punch Owen, had wanted to for the whole trip.

"Well, how stupid do you think I am?" Owen said. He could see that Jeff was about out of patience.

"Well fine then," said Owen, "I guess we can finish this the right way. You can't be right about everything. So maybe you can put your money where your mouth is, like any other man. I can see five cards. If I'm wrong, you going to give me that Mauser rifle you got?"

Jeff started to say something, but Owen had

suddenly placed the rifle in the argument. He thought for an instant about that; he would never have bet the rifle under any other circumstances but he knew he was right. He was mad enough to black both Owen's eyes with one punch. No matter, he was right. He looked one more time at the cards. Then he pushed them up to Owen's face.

"In fact, I will!" he yelled. "You count em. Two and two makes four, you moron!"

Jeff suddenly realized that Owen was smiling from ear to ear. Something was up. He stopped talking and stared at Owen. When he realized what had happened his eyes widened to half again their normal size.

"No!" he yelled.

He scrambled to where he had left the rifle. It wasn't there. Domingo had it. He was holding it with his outstretched arm behind him.

"Sorry Jeff," Domingo said. "You made a deal. I heard it. It's Owen's now."

"Are you crazy?" Jeff yelled, "It was a trick. You

two are in this together, ain't ya? Well, it ain't right. You know what that gun's worth. You think I'm goin' to just give it up to this idiot. He ain't no one."

"You should of thought about that a little while ago," Domingo said. "Right now it's his." Domingo handed the rifle to Owen.

"Don't say no more," Domingo warned Owen. "Just take it and make your bed roll."

Jeff looked from one to the other of the men. He was ready to ride out of camp and never look back. If he could have, he would have considered using a gun to get the rifle back, but he didn't have one.

Jeff was in shock as he watched Owen walk away with his rifle. The realization that he had lost it slowly soaked in. What's worse, he lost it legitimately. Sure Owen had played him, but he fell for it. It was a fool's trick, a trick that left him feeling like a fool.

Owen slept with the rifle in his bedroll with him. He didn't trust Jeff not to take it and run. If he did, Owen worried that he might still use it to kill Three

Feathers. He could shoot that thing from a lot farther than any of them could with what they had. He wasn't sure what he would do with such a rifle, but he was pretty sure Jeff wouldn't be shooting anybody with it.

He was a little surprised the trick had worked. He knew Jeff was a little unstable. He had seen a lot of men like him before. They live on the edge all the time. Pushing them over never takes that much. It helped that Jeff looked down on him to start with, but the trick seemed so simple. Now he would have to watch his back, but he already rode tail. He would just have to keep things that way. He smiled and drifted off to sleep.

Chapter 18

Rabbit in a Trap

When Talon woke up, a small red fox had wandered into his camp. It was sitting with its head cocked a little watching him sleep. He wasn't surprised, he had seen fox do things like that before. The young ones were almost fearless at times. Talon smiled and sat up. When he did, the little fox moved off into the brush and disappeared.

First light was just starting to creep over the tops of the mountains that the canyon ran through. It would soon be where he was. Morning had come later than he wished. Heavy dark clouds overhung the sky and humidity was heavy in the air.

Looking around, he spotted his horses. They were looking for more grass along the stream and on the sides of the canyon. He sat by his bedroll and listened. Nothing out of the ordinary fell to his ears.

A songbird started up and he heard something small skittering through the underbrush. It was the size of a mouse. A sudden movement in the brush suggested that the little fox had breakfast. Talon set out to find something for himself.

He was still not confident enough to build a campfire. He didn't need one anyway. The posse camp had provided well for him. Hardtack and smoked pork. It was fast and easy, nothing to cook. As soon as light was in the canyon Talon was on the trail.

The canyon began to wind back and forth and drop in elevation. He noticed that the sides were coming in as well. By noon, he was being forced to pick his way around large borders and cross the stream back and forth to keep moving.

There was never a place where he could see very far ahead. What he could see wasn't good. Ponderosa pine and wild Juniper trees grew thick in the buffalo grass along the sides of the canyon. Smooth round stones scattered among large boulders made up the floor of the canyon and the bottom kept dropping. He was getting worried about finding a way out. If he could have seen the top he at least could know if there was a way through the rim rock at the top, but the top was altogether out of sight. Anyplace where the trees provided a little break, heavy fog had settled in the upper elevations.

Things were not looking good. If he had to turn back it would mean half a day's ride back to where he had last seen a break in the rim that might by usable. He hoped that wouldn't happen.

After another few hundred feet he stopped to listen. There was a roar of water just ahead. A hundred feet more and he was looking down at a ten-foot drop of water in front of him. After a careful search, it became obvious that there was no way down on horseback. The worst had happened. Talon turned the big gelding back up the trail and stepped out fast.

If he was being followed by the posse, they couldn't be more than a couple hours behind him. If they were pushing hard, they could be closer yet. Staying in the trail he rode at a slow trot. Wearing out the horses at this point would be a very bad idea. After a mile or so, he was forced to slow to a walk.

The paint had long legs and could out-walk the packhorse. She slowed him down. He had to keep pulling her into a trot to make her stay up with the larger horse. In the end, there was nothing to do but keep moving as fast as possible and stay alert.

It was over an hour later when his horse's ears shot forward. Talon stopped in the trail to look. The packhorse was also alert to something in the canyon ahead. How far ahead, he couldn't tell. He sat still and listened. That was when he heard what the horses knew was there; the sound of iron horseshoes on the rocks of the path. They were close, not more than a quarter mile ahead. He was trapped. The canyon wasn't wide enough to get around them on the bottom. He could feel the panic building and shut it down with the memory that fear is a choice. He needed logic now.

The posse would stay in the bottom because his tracks were there. The only hope he could think of was to try to get around them. If he used the thick sides of the canyon he might be able to sit tight and wait for them to pass. Even then, he would have to ride hard and fast to save himself.

There was a boulder in the path large enough that someone coming down the trail could not see over it. Talon left the trail on the downside of the boulder and as close to it as he could. From there he went up the canyon wall. The bank was far too steep to go straight up, and he was forced to ride at a steep angle to gain elevation. After a good climb, he started into fog still hanging in the air from the night before. That was a good thing. If they didn't hear him, he might slip past in the cover of the fog and thick trees.

When he had pushed his horses as hard as he dared, he stopped for a short break. The sun was breaking through the clouds and had been for a while. It was burning off some of the fog. A break in the fog drifted past where Talon was. He stopped and could see the canyon floor below.

What he saw stopped his heart. He had been climbing the wall while at the same time the canyon behind him had been dropping. The natural climb of the canyon on the way out, in front of him, had given him a false impression of his height above the trail. He wasn't more than a hundred feet above the floor.

Straight below where he was Tony was leading the posse past. Talon froze. There was a little wind in the canyon and it blew the long limbs of the Ponderosa trees around enough to help disguise his presence. He was sure that at any second his horses would start a conversation with the posse horses.

He waited and prayed to the Great Spirit that his horse would not alert the riders. To his amazement, none of the horses were in a conversational mood. It was a welcome break. One by one the posse rode by.

Talon watched in silence until they were far enough ahead for him to feel safe, and then he started out again. He was dropping onto the trail when his horse suddenly stopped. Talon had been looking over his shoulder to where he last saw the riders.

When he spun around to see what had stopped the paint, he was looking at Owen Underhill ten feet away. He was caught. There was nothing he could do but wait. Owen was as surprised as Talon. He had come to a stop in the trail and was staring at Talon. Owen raised his right hand in a motion to wait before he spoke.

"Don't shoot," Owen said, "I ain't up to no trouble. I don't care one wit about that saddle, kid. What I need you got with you. I ain't got no time to explain a lot. Just listen, okay. Janice Clanton gave you a scarf. She told me she did. A most beautiful one at that, silk from china. You might believe me to be nuts, but I need it back. It was mine to start with an I ain't got time to explain bout that.

"It's just that my daddy got that from my mom, and he gave it to Bailey on his death bed. That there scarf is the only thing that ties me and Bailey to our papa. If Bailey ever knew I found some way to lose that scarf it would bout kill him."

Owen was talking so fast that Talon had to concentrate to keep up with him.

"Janice," Talon said. He was taken back by the whole conversation. In a way, it wouldn't surprise him if she had used him for something. Especially if she didn't think anyone would ever know, but it was crazy on every level.

He knew how far back the posse was and he knew he was out of time before he started. He would have to think it through later. Owen's words began to soak in.

"Yes," Owen said, "me an her. Well never mind about all that. She was mad, still is. Anyway you do have it, right?"

Owen was getting more desperate all the time. Talon was just staring at him. He looked to be in a state of shock. Owen looked nervously down the trail ahead and then back to Talon.

"Just look at it kid; it has my initials in the corner of it. Same name my dad had. It's an O inside a U, stitched right in."

Owen was running out of time. The last thing he wanted was to get caught by Domingo and the others. A man could get fifteen years in prison for adultery, and Owen knew it. He didn't have time to convince Talon of anything, but he knew he had the scarf.

There was no way for Owen to know how far ahead the posse would go before they started back on Talon's tracks again and found him. Then he remembered the Mauser.

Reaching behind himself he quickly pulled his packhorse forward and pulled it from the pack. Talon's pack had drifted far enough forward that Owen was able to stuff the rifle into his pannier and push it down till it showed only the last half of the stock. Talon watched in amazement.

"There," said Owen. "It's yours. It's a fine rifle. Is it a trade or not?"

Talon remembered the rifle from his visit to their camp and supposed that it belonged to the guard. No matter now, he was pinched for time. Getting rid of Owen looked like it was going to be easy. That said nothing of the posse. He thought for just an instant about keeping the scarf but quickly realized the trade Owen was offering.

The posse horses were clattering down the side of the canyon and Talon knew he needed to fight or run. Owen had the path blocked. He was between a large pine, and a horse sized bolder.

In a panic, he reached into his pannier and found the scarf. Looking over his shoulder for the posse he handed it to Owen. Owen heaved a sigh of relief and bid a quick farewell. As he headed back up the trail he spoke over his shoulder. Bout that posse kid, don't run. All they want is the hangin man's boots.

Talon had been ready to bolt past Owen and

make tracks. He pulled up short and tried to grasp what Owen had just said. He was still struggling with it when Tony called out to him in the language of the Nez Perce. He spun the paint around to meet the approaching posse. The posse was forty feet away, and a little higher than Talon. Owen had disappeared up the canyon.

"No harm," Tony said. "No one is shooting for you." Tony wasn't sure that Talon could understand him. He had no way of knowing what nation Talon belonged to, but he knew that a lot of the words were shared. He also knew that sign language was the universal method of communication between all nations.

He held his right hand with his palm open as far as he could reach up and out toward Talon. It was a gesture to show that he was not holding a weapon. Talon's mind was still sorting out the events of the last few minutes. He was all but in a daze. He understood what Tony had said from his uncle who knew some of the language of the Nez Perce. It told him that he was looking at one of the people he had gone in search of.

Domingo stopped cold. He knew that they were close, and had prepared himself for anything. He could see the earth and small rock still coming loose and falling in Talon's horse's tracks. The side they were on was steep and loose. That made it easy to stay in his tracks. It also let him know that they were only minutes behind him. What he was expecting was a chase.

He had the thought that they might even find themselves in a gunfight. What he never expected was to ride up on him face on. The surprise caught him off guard.

"Take it easy now kid," Domingo yelled. "Nobody moves."

He looked back to his posse. "Stand your ground. I'll shoot any man that pulls a gun." It was a knee-jerk reaction he realized was a fool's statement as soon as he said it, but it was all he could think of.

Talon remembered the ammunition and smiled. It put him a little at ease. *Of course, they won't pull a gun,* he thought, *I have all their bullets.*

Domingo's eyes dropped to Talon's foot. He wasn't wearing the boots. For a moment he worried they had chased the wrong man. He trusted Tony; the only tracks they had seen led to Talon. It had to be the right man. He looked for Owen. He would know if this was the one they called Three Feathers. If it was, he was not involved. Owen wasn't with the rest of the posse.

"Owen," called Domingo.

"Here," Owen said. He had moved back up behind Talon again. It seemed to Domingo that Owen was taking that tail position a little too seriously, but he didn't take time to think it through.

"This your man?" Domingo asked.

"Owen pointed at Talon and nodded his head yes.

Talon was surrounded. He had no choice but to wait for the next thing. Owen was no threat, but he had put himself in the way again. Jeff was disappointed. His opportunity had been missed. Domingo looked back at Talon.

"You found a hanging man?" Domingo asked.

Talon nodded.

"You got the boots?"

Talon nodded again. Domingo sighed a breath of relief.

"You ain't in no trouble. All I need is those boots you got off the hangin man. They're the only evidence I got in a murder case. It could explode without them."

Domingo had thought long and hard about whether or not Talon could have been involved in the shooting of Brodie Buckhart. Owen had given him the clue he needed. He had mentioned the timeline of his encounter with Talon at the shop. There was no way Talon could have been involved. He was with the Clantons at the time of the shooting. He didn't leave town until later that morning.

At this point, all Domingo wanted was the evidence that the Buckhart boys had hung the right man.

Talon's head was spinning. He liked the boots, but if that's all the posse wanted, he had been running for nothing. But was it? Was Domingo telling it straight, or was he thinking that Talon was involved? If so, he might be trying to get closer and take him in a hand to hand fight. After all, if they had any ammunition left it was very little.

He looked over at Tony. Tony looked down at Talon's buckskin moccasin, then back to Talon. He nodded. Talon didn't know Tony but he hoped he wouldn't sell him out. He pulled the pack mare up to where he was and fished around in the panniers until he found the boots. They were fine boots. He hated to give them up. Domingo stepped his horse forward and Talon gave him the boots.

"That's all?" Talon asked.

"Unless you know something I don't, that's all," said Domingo.

Talon was still in a bit of shock. He had been running for nothing. Owen even turned out to be a non-event. In a way, he felt stupid. In another, relieved. He looked at the rest of the men around him. They were all staring at him like they were expecting him to do something. Then he thought of the ammunition and decided to lighten his load a little more.

He pulled his leather pack out of the pannier and held it open to Domingo. It had all the ammunition he had taken from their guns. Domingo smiled and began collecting the cartridges out of the pack. He handed them around to the posse.

He found the eight-millimeter rounds and held them in his hand, then looked over to Owen. Owen had a bit of a sheepish smile on his face. It was only then that Domingo noticed that the butt of the Mauser was not sticking out of Owen's saddle pack. He also noticed that Talon had two stocks sticking out of his.

Domingo didn't know what had gone down, but he didn't care. He looked at Talon and dropped the cartridges back into the pack. For a moment no one spoke. It had been a long ride and it had ended like a rifle shot. Domingo was glad. He had what he came for, and without any blood on the ground.

"One thing," Talon said, on your way back home

you should stop in the camp I visited. The rest of
your supplies are buried next to the large willow
tree in the creek bank."

"Well that's good to know," Domingo said. He
touched the brim of his hat and bumped his heels
into the flanks of his horse.

Talon shifted his horses a little off trail and let
the posse past. One by one they joined Owen on
the trail back up the canyon. Tony was the last to
pass by. He stopped when he got next to Talon. He
wanted to meet him. In a way, he felt that he already
knew him. He had analyzed his every move for the
better part of two weeks. It told him what kind of
man he was after.

Talon was no threat to Tony, but he was a curiosity. Another intriguing thing was that he was close
to home. Talon had been heading in the direction of
his people for the entire trip, almost like he knew
where he was going and was aiming for the Nez
Perce nation.

"You goin north?" Tony asked.

Talon was a little surprised that he had stopped to ask. The rest of the posse was still moving up the trail.

"I think north a little more. Mostly west maybe, I am looking for your people."

Tony had been right. Talon was trying to get to the Nez Perce reservation. He wondered why. Talon wasn't Nez Perce. What's more, he didn't know where the reservation was.

"You mean the Nez Perce?" Tony asked. "Why my people?"

"They are holding land of mine. Can you take me there?"

Tony had been thinking of the trail home. He had even entertained the idea of not going back with the posse. His thought was maybe to go home for a visit and then return to Wolf Creek later, but the city owed him now and it was money he needed.

"I would like to," Tony said, "but they owe me money." He nodded his head up the trail as he said it.

Talon knew what Tony was saying was true. He also knew that he would have a much harder time finding the cabin without him. He tried to think of a way to convince Tony to take him on to his people. He didn't have time to explain why he wanted to go. That would have at least helped.

The thought came to him that even if he could just get information from Tony, it would help. He thought of going back with the posse to where they would end the day and camp but that seemed too uncomfortable to him. Anyway, it would take two days off his direction.

Then he thought of the Mauser. He didn't need it and in the end, would have sold it. Or even been killed for it. He reached into his pack and handed the rifle to Tony.

"This pay enough?"

Tony smiled and took the eight-millimeter from Talon. He had been looking at it. It had occurred to him that Talon might part with it. He hoped he might offer it to him for payment.

Riding for the posse was easy. He would be riding somewhere anyway. Getting a rifle like the

Mauser was out of his reach. Under any other circumstances, he knew he could never own one. The
thought of riding into the land of his own people
with such a prize was a proud thought. He would be
respected by anyone who saw it. It was a good trade.

"We need to catch up," Tony said. I need to tell
Sheriff Wells. Then we will go."

Tony rode ahead of Talon at a trot. In a quarter
mile, he had caught back up with Domingo.

"Domingo," he called out. Domingo stopped his
horse and turned to look at Tony.

"I'm not going with you back to town," Tony
said. Domingo looked at Tony and then back to
Talon. Tony had the rifle now. It was making its
rounds.

"Well," said Domingo "I guess we can get back
without you. You can do what you want, I
suppose."

He would have liked to have asked questions,
but what was on his mind wasn't really his business
anyway, and in the end, it wouldn't matter. He want-

ed and needed to be on his way.

"I owe you money, Tony. Well, the city does anyway."

Tony was holding the Mauser in his right hand. The rifle butt was rested against the saddle horn. Jeff was staring at it and then at Owen. Tony and Owen were both smiling. Owen had no idea how Tony had acquired it but he guessed that Three Feathers had just hired a guide. Jeff glared back over at Tony.

"You want I should send it someplace?" Domingo asked.

Tony thought for a moment. He was staring at Jeff and grinning.

"No," Tony said. "Give it to Jeff. He needs to start saving for another fancy rifle. Owen laughed out loud. Jeff spun his horse around and started off alone down the trail. Domingo just chuckled and waved goodbye.

"Your call," he said over his shoulder.

CHAPTER 19

MEANWHILE, BACK AT THE RANCH

Talon had lost the boots and the beautiful scarf. He still had a new hat though, and it would go nicely with his new clothes. He took it off and brushed a little dust off the brim. He also had a new friend, one who would make his trip a lot easier. He put the hat back on and thought of the trail ahead. Then he remembered the trail behind him.

The place where he was in his journey seemed like a place of change, like he was moving away from something that would never be again. He thought momentarily of his new clothes, also of the Clantons.

They were part of how he came to this place.

He thought of Janice and shook his head. In a way, it didn't surprise him much. In another way, it was a slap in the face. She had used him like a child. Then he thought of Lacey and wondered if she really had tried to follow him. In the end that didn't matter much either, but he did feel a little sorry for her. Then on second thought, he decided that if he had ever met a woman who could take care of herself, Lacey was the woman.

What he couldn't know, was that Lacey had tried to follow him. She rode home with Ed and Janice the night they left Wolf Creek. When she felt safe, she had slipped out of the cabin back door. Skirting the cabin, she made her way in the moonlight to the corral where the two mares were.

She had planned on trying to leave for a month before Talon had arrived. Her plan had always involved using the mares but she had no way to know how she might break them. Talon had solved that problem.

Ed bought the horses long before Talon had showed up at the ranch. The minute Lacey saw them she knew what she wanted to do. Every spare moment after they arrived had been spent getting them used to her presence. She hand fed them anything they seemed to like and they were used to her petting their noses and as far up their necks as she could reach. She was afraid to try to get into the corral with them, but that too would change in time.

The night she left, she packed one bundle of clothes and entered the corral. When she caught the lead rope of the sorrel, she led her to the gate-post Talon had used to break her.

She had no idea how she would find Talon, or if she could. For now, it was enough to just be getting away. When she had the sorrel tied to the corral, she tried to tie the pack onto her back. The little mare tolerated her attempt to get it secure without moving. When she finished, her pack looked like a tangled wad of yarn but it was the best she could do. She had no pack saddle. The bay by then had become used to the saddle. She was no problem to saddle up.

The first hundred yards or so of her escape went as planned. She had her horses and was headed back to Wolf Creek. Then the trouble started.

First, the pack slid under the little sorrel and made her start crow-hopping and kicking. That put her ahead of the bay and forced Lacey to turn the bay in a circle to keep the sorrel from cutting her off and tangling the horses in the lead rope.

The sorrel made three full circles kicking and fighting the rope. In the process, she kicked the little bundle of clothes open and scattered them on the ground under her feet. Only then did she stop fighting long enough to let Lacey off the bay. When she got off her horse to salvage her pack and try again, the bay tried to leave without her. She caught the bay again and finally got started back down the road.

She had not gone any distance, when the sorrel, who was not comfortable with the pack, trotted past the bay again and once again, Lacey turned a tight circle in the direction away from the sorrel to keep them from getting tangled. Then the pack fell down again and had to be fixed.

It never occurred to Lacey to pull the packhorse up close to the bay until she had no room to pull forward. The shorter lead rope would have forced her to comply.

Another thing that had never occurred to her was that she had left without any camp supplies. The plan looked good in her mind. She would just get the now-broke horses and use the smaller one for a pack. That had been Talon's idea, but that's not how it was going.

Lacey was still fighting the horses when the sun came up and she was only a few miles from home. The thought came to her how good it was that she had no gun. She had become frustrated enough to shoot one of them.

The bay was green and could not neck rein. Trying to hold the lead rope and plow-rein the

mare was nearly impossible, but not a deal break-
er. By the time the sun was climbing in the sky, she
had the two horses worked into a froth and was
nearly in tears.

Frustrated to near defeat, she had come to a stop
in the middle of the road just over a small rise high
enough to hide her back trail. The pack had fallen
again and she was standing beside the horse, not
knowing what she could do about it. She was about
to scream in anger when she realized someone had
ridden up on her and was sitting on his horse thirty
feet away. It was Ed.

"Don't say nothin till you hear me out," he told
her. "I figured this day might come. I could see it
buildin for a while. That's the most reason I decided
not to break those two knotheads you got there myself. Wasn't sure how I would handle that.

"Anyway, I ain't mad. In fact, I don't blame you.
I might do the same. So now here we are. As you
must have noticed, I ain't the man your ma wanted
me to be. She puts on her war paint every morning,

and I don't do much to make things any better. Still, you have to think we do our best."

Then Ed's voice got serious. "There ain't much I love in this world, Lacey. I can count it all on one hand. In fact, on one finger. You, that's about all. I will do whatever I need to do to keep you as long as I can.

"So, here's my deal. You give me two more years to build the herd. You'll be eighteen by then and a little more settled. In two years that little patch of dust I call a ranch will have a good number of cows on it and if someone hasn't shot me by then, I'll sell the whole thing off and split the money three ways. Even split.

"You can leave in style Lacey, like a lady should. I won't want it anyway without you on it. Just give me two more years, and all three of us can go our separate ways and have a good start somewhere else."

Lacey thought about what Ed told her and agreed to go back, at least for another two years, but, true to her word, she really had tried to follow Talon and she would again. Somehow she would follow him, and he would lead her to the rest of her life. She was sure of it.

Chapter 20

The Trail Ends

Tony and Talon climbed out of the canyon at their first opportunity. Tony changed Talon's course a little and headed more west. The day held the promise of a good ride. They held to the ridge for a few miles and then dropped into another valley. This one was wide and had a lot of other little canyons that fed into it. It was timbered and once they started down into it all that could be seen were the trees and underbrush.

The trails Tony used were game trails that came and went. Small springs with green grass seemed to develop out of nowhere and were gone just as fast.

There were less rocks and more sagebrush. The canopy of the pines overhead kept the sun from finding most of the forest floor and allowed for mushrooms and ferns to take root. Talon had never seen mushrooms like some of these. They looked like they might be good to eat.

By mid-afternoon, the thick forest of Ponderosa and fir trees had given way to juniper and brush.

They left the big valley and were working a narrow trail along the edge of a prairie flat. The flat bordered the tree line of a small range of mountains. It stretched as far as Talon could see on his left. On his right were tall Ponderosa and rich smelling Juniper. The smells of the trees mingled with the smell of the blooming sagebrush and meadow grass islands that happened here and there along the way. This was the essence of life to Talon. The scent from the horse blankets mingled with the smell of the fresh green grass as they made their way along. It was a good day. The warm sun and fresh air felt like the song he had in his heart.

All seemed well. Talon was no longer feeling like he needed to be looking over his shoulder, though he often did anyway. It had become a habit he adopted as a boy. Now and then, the saddle creaked and it too sounded like the music of good fortune. Soon enough, his mind came back to the task at hand.

He began to wonder what kind of person Tony might turn out to be. They had not taken time to talk yet. Talon was riding behind him and Tony had not said anything.

Tony held the rifle up a few times and looked through the scope. Then he used his shirttail to polish its bright blued surface to a sheen. Talon was glad that he liked it. He hoped he hadn't offended Tony by taking his ammunition while he slept. Now that he depended on him to guide, he needed to feel he could trust that he would not leave in the night.

The end of the day found them crossing one of the little well-watered meadows. It was the end of a very good day. The soft whisper of the horses' legs passing through the tall grass and muffled plodding of their hooves in the rich meadow soil, made for a peaceful feeling as they watched the sun setting on the path in front of them. Songbirds flitted through the trees in search of suitable roosts. While off on the prairie some distance away, a coyote howled in his celebration of a warm night to come.

They camped that night in a brush flat along a clear stream. Ahead of them loomed a mountain range that stood tall and straight. It was covered with forest, and the distant tops were still white with snow. Talon hoped Tony knew a way into it. From where they camped, it looked like it was either straight up or straight down.

The supplies Talon had taken would not last as long with two men to feed. A day for hunting might become necessary. Talon thought of setting a snare for a small animal but decided against it. They still had enough for a few days. He built a small fire and set a couple cans of beans near the coals to heat, then he waited for the bean juice to heat enough to bubble out through the holes he had punched in the tops of the cans.

Tony rolled his bed out and sat on it to watch the fire. He was curious about what Talon had said at the waterfall. Talon had said that the Nez Perce people were holding land for him. The only land he could remember was reservation land. Another thing he wondered about was why Owen Underhill called him Three Feathers. That could wait. He didn't want to ask too many questions too soon.

The first thing he decided he wanted to know was Talon's real name. "Did I say that my name is Tony Blackhawk?" Tony asked.

Talon thought for a second. He had been riding all day with Tony and couldn't remember if he had even heard Tony's name. "I don't remember; good to know though. My name is Talon. I am of the Windcatcher people of the Lakota."

Tony's head suddenly raised to meet Talon's eyes. He had a concerned look in his eyes. For a moment he was silent. Talon felt the tension and said nothing.

"Windcatcher, I know that name. My people talk of it from time to time. It is a long time since I heard it. The land you speak of is the place we call spirit house." He reached over and picked up the rifle. His hands caressed the fine rifle one more time. Then he handed it to Talon. "I will not take you there." He said

Talon thought for a moment. He needed Tony and he already liked him. He pushed the rifle, still in Tony's hand back at him. "Do you know the way to the spirit house?"

"Not many of my people do, but I do. It is forbidden even now to go there. We are not even allowed to talk of it anymore. Most people would not understand why. I understand." He rested the butt of the rifle on the ground but kept it upright, still offering it to Talon.

"You have seen it?" asked Talon.

"Yes, I was young; my father took me up the river the whites call Clearwater. It is one of our rivers. We were hoping for beaver. It was late in the fall.

The snow had not come in high country yet, so we made camp and went to look for the beaver.

"We worked hard, and my father was tired when he went to sleep. He had showed me the place of the house of stones earlier in the day. When he slept I slipped from camp and wanted to see it closer. I was only a boy.

"Our medicine man had warned that if we disturbed the spirits they would visit our people again and death would come with them. I knew this about the lodge of stone so I wanted to be very careful not to go inside.

"I walked up the Clearwater to the river called Oxbow and there it was. It was a full moon night. I remember an owl was perched on the roof of the house. He stayed even when I was close enough to see his eyes in the light of the moon. I was already very afraid. He didn't need to do that. I walked very slowly to the door of the cabin. I was waiting to see if the spirits would be disturbed. I listened very closely."

His voice quickened as he spoke. "Suddenly

the house moaned at me and I felt its cold breath on my feet." He paused for a second. The memory was still fresh in his mind and not pleasant. His eyes went from staring at the fire to suddenly looking up at Talon. They were wide with fear and stared directly into Talon's.

"It was calling me to come in." He said earnestly. "I wanted to run but the spirits had hold of my feet and they would not move. I was about to call out to the Great Spirit when the house spoke again. It was a tortured sounding, long moan, like the moan of a man who could no longer speak. "As it moaned, its breath blew cold again against my feet."

He looked again at the fire. Talon could hear the fear in Tony's voice. "I tell you, it blew dust at me and cried for me to come in. All of my strength was not enough to free me. Finally, I thought of my father, and when my mind had gone to our camp it had no hold on me and I ran.

"A few days after we came home, the wife of a medicine man died. She was not well when we left, so I could never be sure, but it was enough. I can not take you to the spirit house. They will remember me."

Tony sat Indian fashion on the ground with the rifle still held out and stared at Talon. He was determined that he would not go. Not even if he had to give up the great rifle.

Talon thought of what he had told him. He could see that Tony was genuine in his heart and that he would not take him. In truth, he was more afraid of the cabin now himself. Now he had met a man who had seen the cabin and was an eye witness to the spirits that lived there. Still, he reasoned, even if I don't use the cabin, the land is still mine and I can build another one. "How close will you take me?"

Tony thought of the place. He had not been there for a long time. The town of Cougar Rock was only a trading post in those days. He remembered that to get to the town it was necessary to cross the Clearwater River between the Big Bear Valley and the trading post if you approached from the north.

They would be coming from the south.

He remembered that if you came from the north, you could follow the river up that side and go to the cabin that way. It was a much rougher route and required that you do a lot of climbing of small hills that the river ran up against or cut off leaving small cliffs of loose ground that eroded away a little every spring. The best way was to go to Cougar Rock and cross the river there. The cabin was on the north side of the river. From the trading post, you would cross at a braided place in the river. On the other side, there was a trail that was well used by game.

"I will take you to the little trading post at Cougar Rock. It is close to the place you seek. I will tell you how to get to the place from there. It is about five miles from the trading post. I will not go closer. "Do you know the spirits are real? They might visit your people, or even mine if you disturb them, but I think it more likely it will be yours. Still, if you want to go, then go, but you will go alone."

Talon nodded his head and pushed the rifle back

toward Tony again. Tony smiled and cradled it in his arms like a child. To Talon the Mauser had become the key to the door of his future. To Tony, it was the pride of his life. He could hardly wait to show it to his brother and sisters on the reservation.

First light found the two men in their saddles and headed more north than west. The trail Tony chose worked up a long draw and then switched back and forth up the mountains into the high valleys. Once on the top, he stayed there for as many days as he could.

The reservation started in high country but included a lot of open land as well. It followed the valley of the Clearwater and was rich and wild.

They traveled along many high mountain tops and down into small river valleys. The game became plentiful and the trees were larger here than any place Talon had ever seen. He had never seen grouse either, but here they were all over the mountains. They were smaller than the sage hens he was used to and flew faster.

Tony knew the country, and he stayed to the best passes and crossings. Summer was at its hottest days when they crossed into reservation land and Tony could begin to feel home. They camped that night on a dry grassy knoll with a south wind pushing to go home. Tony would have ridden on, knowing that his village was not far. They would be there easily before noon the next day. He thought of it but decided to wait till morning and not find everyone asleep when he arrived there.

It was getting dark when they rolled out their bedrolls and slept. They were down to what they caught in the snares for food. It wasn't bad, but Tony began to remember the food his family would have. Salmon might still be in the Salmon River, and if so they would be feasting on them, or maybe elk. He remembered the tenderloin of the elk and got too excited to sleep. In the morning, he would be home again. He would see his little sister. She was a child, and cried when he left. He remembered other things as well and finally slipped into sleep smiling.

Talon was awakened by the sound of Tony rolling his bedroll and putting his few belongings into his panniers. The sun wasn't up yet, but the distant hills were showing a dim bar of light across their tops. Coyotes were howling as they often did in the first light of day. They were usually what woke Talon up. They ate a cold breakfast and were on the trail before the sun knew they were there.

The lay of the land had become more of a flat plain. It was about midday, and Talon could see a good river in the distance, as they dropped down off a little rise they had climbed only moments before. Once on top, Tony stopped and looked down. Talon rode up beside him and could see what he was looking at.

On the downhill side of the little rise was a small village. It was on the flat just at the bottom of the hill and was built on the banks of a good spring that disappeared into the grassland beyond. There was one cabin and several lodges on it. Smoke rose from the cabin and one of the lodges that was a few hundred yards from the cabin. It drifted high into the sunny sky and faded away.

Someone must be preparing a noonday meal, thought Talon. It was another sign that he was in a land of plenty. Most people in his village back home ate only once a day some days. Rich days they ate two times, but very rarely three.

A man about Tony's age came out of the cabin and started walking toward the spring. Children were playing in the water and Talon could hear them laughing.

Tony smiled over at Talon and dropped the lead rope for his packhorse. At the same time, he brought his heels into his horse's flank hard and started off in a full gallop. When the man by the spring heard the thunder of the horse's hooves he tried to run for the cabin but was not fast enough. Tony screamed a war hoop and landed on top of him. The horse ran on a few feet as the two men wrestled in the dry grass.

In a few seconds, the man Tony had attacked jumped to his feet and yelled "Tony!" He jumped onto Tony again, but now they were standing. A young man ran from the cabin with a rifle but when he saw who had come, he dropped it and ran to one of the lodges. It was the lodge with the cooking fire. Almost as soon as he ran into it yelling Tony's name, a young woman ran out. She was dressed in a doe-skin dress and knee high moccasins. She was scream-ing Tony's name and she ran like the wind.

The two men were laughing and talking excited-ly when she got to where they were. She threw her-self at Tony with such force that she nearly knocked him off his feet. He wrapped his arms around her and squeezed with all his might.

Talon later learned that her name was Spring Snow and she was Tony's little sister, the one who had cried when he left. She was seventeen now and had a child of her own. She was very beautiful. Her waist-long, jet-black hair blew over Tony's shoulder and down his back when she flew into his arms. Her feet were off the ground and Tony spun her round and round. They were saying something in Nez Perce but Talon could only catch part of it. She was crying again, this time for joy.

The night came with laughter and songs. Children played games and Tony played one game with them. It was a game with a loop made of willow that was kept rolling by the use of a stick used to strike the top of it much the way one might roll a rim. The idea was to steal the loop without touching it and get to your side of the court for a score.

It was a night to remember, and people from other small villages across the reservation soon arrived. The young man Talon had seen earlier had gone to tell them the good news.

The man Tony had tackled was his brother. He was very impressed with the Mauser. "You have become very rich," he told Tony. They fired it, but only once. Ammunition would not be easy to get, and Tony only had a few rounds.

Talon was introduced, but the cabin was not mentioned. Tony only said that they were going to Cougar Rock, and Tony would leave Talon there. Some of Tony's family said that Talon should live with them.

It was a tempting thought, but he had other plans.

The next day, Talon spent two hours riding through the village looking at the Palouse River horses the Nez Perce raised. They had founded the breed and were the first known people in North America to practice controlled breeding. The name Appaloosa came later. It was the name that Talon had heard them called.

He had seen only a few of the horses on his way through Wolf Creek. These were the most beautiful horses he had ever seen. They were better bred than the ones he had seen before. Their rumps were wider and their lungs were wide and deep. They were formed perfectly, and Talon knew he would someday raise them himself. He had a way into the Nez Perce now, and he would use it.

Tony went to the lodge of the chief of the village and explained in private who Talon was and why he had come. At first, the chief was not willing for Tony to even show him the way. He wanted Tony to give him a map. The argument lasted for over an hour.

The elders were called and they all went into the

council lodge on the bank of the Clearwater. Talon was not allowed to enter there, and even Tony was left outside of the council lodge. The chief took Talon's request to the elders. The land, they agreed, was Talon's and the spirit house as well. However, he would not be allowed to visit any of the Nez Perce for two full years after he took possession of it.

If the spirits were real, Talon would be gone by then. If the spirits had left or were forever sleeping, then it would be safe for him to visit the Nez Perce again. A document of agreement and ownership of the land would be left at the general store in a few days by a carrier. The carrier was not allowed to meet with Talon personally.

Cougar Rock was less than two days from the Reservation. A good man on one of the Appaloosa horses could make the trip in about twelve hours if he rode hard. A lot of Nez Perce had begun to trade in Cougar Rock and the way there was well known. Talon could have found it without any trouble himself, but Tony had made a deal and he stuck to that deal.

CHAPTER 21

WELCOME HOME MOANED THE WIND

It was midday on the day that the two men arrived at Cougar rock, and they stopped just outside town. The road into town had a large
ponderosa pine in it, at the edge of town, and one
needed to go around it to enter Cougar Rock.
Tony and Talon shook hands there and the deal
was finished. Tony had a map drawn on a small
piece of doeskin that he gave to Talon. He was sad
that in the very best of conditions, he would not
see Talon for at least two years, but he admired
him for his bravery.

Talon watched Tony ride out of sight before he turned the large paint in the direction of town and bumped his flanks.

Talon rode through Cougar Rock until he came to the general store. Tony had told him to ask the owner for credit in his name to get a grubstake. The owner's name, Tony told him, was Joseph Long. Talon did as Tony had said, and showed the map he had to Joseph. In the corner of the map was a symbol that Tony's family used as a signature and Joseph recognized it.

"So," said Joseph, "you're the one who actually owns that haunted cabin on the Oxbow are ya?"

"Yes sir," said Talon. He wasn't sure how much Information he should volunteer. The cabin already had a bad reputation with the nations. How the white world felt about it was unknown to him, and he thought it best to tread lightly.

"Ya know what they say bout that place, don't ya?" asked Joseph

"Yes sir," said Talon, "I plan to see for myself. It is mine."

Joseph thought about things for a moment before he spoke. "No offense, but are you sure you want to be messin round there? It ain't just the nations that think there might be something strange going on at that place. Some of the locals have ventured over there and they say bout the same thing. The place is just plain creepy.

"Word is, that cabin sounds like wind when there ain't no wind around. One fella even told me that if you stand outside and listen long enough you can hear what sounds like a distant stream or river coming through the walls. At first he thought it was the oxbow but it ain't, he was sure of that. If I was you I think I might reconsider trying to live in it, or even hang around it. Not trying to pry into anyone's business though. Just sayin."

Talon remembered what Tony had told him and it sounded a lot the same. It sent a cold chill down his spine, but he came a long way to see it and he meant to do just that.

"Thanks," said Talon, I'll be careful. "

"You do that," said Joseph. He boxed up Talon's goods and walked him to the door.

When Talon left the store he had enough supplies to last a week. He wasn't sure how he would pay for them, but Joseph told him he could wait until the fur was prime, if need be.

He left town and rode across the river to the trail on the other side. A few miles later he passed by the Stonewell cabin. Joseph had warned him it was there, and that it was not the right one. When he saw it, he knew that he was in the right place and rode on. A short while later, he found the Oxbow River, and from the convergence of the two rivers he could see the cabin. The day was losing light and he thought of making camp for the night in the meadow. The grass there was about two feet tall and grew thick with wildflowers. A light breeze pushed down the river and sent waves through the grass and the sedges along the riverbank. Pine bows cast shadows that danced along the edge of the meadow and the hill behind them.

Talon sat on the large paint and watched the ancient-looking cabin for a long time. Other than the grass in front of it, nothing moved. After a little while, he dismounted and ventured closer to look through the window in the front of the cabin. It was a large window. It seemed odd to him, that such a small cabin would have such a large window. He wondered why.

The inside of the cabin was completely exposed and he could see all the walls inside. It was dusty inside the cabin. The table looked as if it had not been used in a very long time and the stove was in perfect condition except for the dust. It was all there. Under other conditions, he thought the top plates of the stove should be cracked or missing. They were often taken by someone needing to replace the ones that cracked on their own stove.

From outside the cabin, he could see well enough into the small room in front of him to see that the whole cabin seemed to be frozen in time. He noticed that the glass in the window panes was not as flat-looking as he had seen. It seemed to be sort of wavy and had little bubbles in it in places. It was also off-colored a little. It seemed very old.

Nothing seemed out of place or threatening. He remembered what Tony had told him about the cabin moaning. It was on his mind now.

Walking back far enough to see the roof, he looked to see if the owl had returned. It seemed to him that it might not be flesh, maybe a warning spirit of some kind. Tony told him that the Nez Perce believed that the spirits of the dead were in the owls. Talon's people reverenced them as messengers of important news. It could be a warning if one had suddenly shown itself on the roof. There was nothing on the roof.

He was standing in front of the cabin looking up when he heard the moan that Tony had warned him of. His eyes went instantly to the front door of the cabin. He listened intently for a few seconds without moving.

The house moaned again and he realized that the sound came from the door, just the door, not the cabin. In a few seconds, the door moaned again and he heard the door shift in its frame and bump against the jam. He had been afraid before that, but now things seemed to be coming together.

He realized that he had heard the sound of the moaning before. It was in the high mountain tops where boulders were stacked and the wind blew through them. He waited and watched, but the only sound he heard was the sound of the wind around him. Then the moaning happened again. *It's the wind,* thought Talon. He remembered what Joseph had said about it sounding like wind. It must be making that sound because the wind is blowing around the cabin. Where it sits must create moaning in the wind. He walked up to the door and was about to open it when he felt a cool breeze from under the door. It grew into a stronger breeze and then the house moaned again.

Talon dragged his foot over the silted dust on the boards in front of the door. The wind under the door picked it up and blew it over his feet. He realized that the wind never stopped blowing under the door. It only moaned when the wind blew strong enough to make it.

It really is the wind, thought Talon. *It's coming in from some broken place in one of the cabin walls and blowing out under the door.* He reached out and pushed down on the handle that lifted the drop lever inside the house. The door swung open with a creak. Inside was a bare floor. It had been made of pine boards and there were cracks between them. All along the cracks were little ridges of dust the wind had left behind. He stepped into the cabin and looked around.

The room he was in was wall-to-wall rough-cut pine. In one of the floorboards was a perfect round hole. It was about three feet from the door. He walked over to it on the creaking floor and looked down. It looked like it was there to remove part of the floor, so he put his finger into it and lifted. A section of the floor lifted up until it hit the bottom of the entry door. It was a trap door. He lowered it a little and the wind from the trap door closed the entry door with a thud. That unnerved him a little. He waited to see if anything else would happen. Nothing did, so he tried the trap door again. It had no hinges and opened easily. Under it was an ancient ladder made of juniper wood.

That was the day Talon Windcatcher came home. He quickly discovered why people went missing in the cave under the cabin. He discovered that there was gold in the stream that flowed under it. It was not a lot of gold but it would feed him well if he worked it enough. The cave, he soon learned was far bigger than the shaft that he first discovered. He explored it as far as a torch would let him and decided that it was too large and fragmented to be explored safely. No doubt others before him had not been as wise and were still lost and dead somewhere in the mountain. For him it was enough that he had a beautiful valley and an excellent cabin in a rich land. And the spirits, if there were any, were not showing up. For now life was good.

The natural shape and size of the shaft the cabin was built across allowed enough room for living quarters, and that is where he soon settled. The spirit house continued to moan and the dust continued to collect on the little table upstairs, and Talon became part of it as others had before him.

It was indeed a rich land, with grass aplenty, and water clear and clean. It was just as the legend of his people had said. Talon camped in the meadow of the cabin that night and left the door of the cabin tied open, just in case it tried to moan again. At the break of day the next morning Talon's new life dawned with the day.

Did you enjoy this book?

We need your help! Your honest opinion is the most effective tool we have to get the word out about Don's books. Reviews are the number one thing readers rely on when looking at a book by an author they have not read before. If you will take just a few minutes and give your honest opinion of this book on Amazon, Goodreads, or your favorite book site, it will make a huge difference. Thank you.

THE WINDCATCHER'S CAVE

In *The Windcatcher's Cave*, book 2 in the Windcatcher series, Talon and his neighbor Aggie are trapped when she is chased into the cave by a bear with no intention of letting them go.

The long shadow that filled the doorway was all she needed to know that the bear was still behind her. Bruised and dazed she ran for her life into the total darkness of the cave. The dull thud of the bear hitting the ground in the entry let her know he was not giving up.

Aggie Stonewell was not supposed to be there. She was a good girl from a good family, and it was such a harmless little lie. Where it took her was beyond belief. Into miles of interlocking caves, with a man she had only seen from a distance. Feeling their way in the total absence of light, through stone structures and sulfur springs in the deep, dark, dampness of a massive cave whose only sound was the constant wind and the occasional moan of the bear that had nowhere else to be.

In the outside world, the ground echoed with the sound of horses' hooves, scouring every inch of forest for miles, desperate to find a young woman lost someplace in the Sawtooth, a land that rarely gives up it's dead.

Under the Flowers

Under the Flowers is the third and final book in the Windcatcher series.

The day Seth Jackson disappeared was a normal sunny day. Then he was gone - it was like he had never been there in the first place.

The quiet little town of Cougar Rock, Idaho had been a safe place whose greatest worries were the dust and the mosquitoes. Then it hit — and everything happened at once. One man missing without a trace, another one dead, and no one with any answers. At the same time, someone tries to burn down the West Fork Hotel. A beautiful young blond shows up out of nowhere and buys the fire-damaged hotel. Domingo Wells is called in to be sheriff but most of the clues are underground. Some of them in the grave of the dead man, the rest still moving around down there.

All three books in the Windcatcher series are available in paperback, large print and eBook formats, through your favorite bookstore or online retailer. You can visit our website at tazlinaglacier.com for information on purchasing them in person or online.

Staying in Touch

To receive notice when Under the Flowers is released, or any special offers are available, join our email list at https://tazlinaglacier.com/email/

Our publishing company website:

https://tazlinaglacier.com

Donald Hofstetter, Author Facebook page:

https://www.facebook.com/donaldhofstetter/

Don's Instragram page with pictures of Alaska, Idaho, and the things he most enjoyed:

https://www.instagram.com/
donaldhofstetter_alaska_idaho/

Email to: thofstetter@tazlinaglacier.com

www.ingramcontent.com/pod-product-compliance
Lightning Source LLC
Chambersburg PA
CBHW051212120726
47905CB00004B/1090